Angus MacDonald has lived all his life in the Highlands. He served in the local regiment, the Queen's Own Highlanders, before building a financial publishing company that was sold in 2007. He now has businesses in recycling, renewables and education, and runs the Moidart Trust, a charitable organisation that helps people to develop companies in the West Highlands. He is married to Michie and has four sons – Archie, Jack, Jamie and Donald.

Ardnish Was Home

ANGUS MACDONALD

Sarah

fond regards

Angus MacDonald

BIRLINN

First published in 2016 by
Birlinn Limited
West Newington House
10 Newington Road
Edinburgh
EH9 1QS

www.birlinn.co.uk

5

ISBN: 978 1 78027 426 3

British Library Cataloguing-in-Publication Data
A catalogue record for this book is
available from the British Library

Typeset by Hewer Text UK Ltd, Edinburgh
Printed and bound by MBM Print SCS Ltd, Glasgow

MIX
Paper from
responsible sources
FSC® C117931

Acknowledgements and Dedication

Ardnish Was Home started as a short story and grew and grew. Holidays, starting at the millennium and for the next sixteen years, saw me rise ridiculously early and write for a few hours until we headed out to play. In between I would be collecting and collating the stories.

As my siblings and I were being reared in the West Highlands, our father was the non-stop fount of these anecdotes, and we participated in the old ways of clipping the sheep, the gathering, stalking deer and building hay stacks. My grandfather would regale us with stories of his father, Colonel Willie, who plays a key role. It was my father too, who on reading the first few thousand words, encouraged me to persevere and complete the book.

So, thanks to my father, Rory MacDonald, to whom I dedicate *Ardnish Was Home*, for providing both the tales and the inspiration to write it.

AM

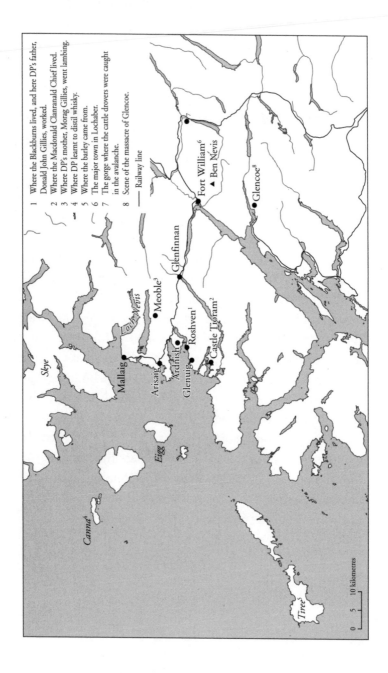

1 Where the Blackburns lived, and here DP's father,
   Donald John Gillies, worked.
2 Where the Macdonald Clanranald Chief lived.
3 Where DP's mother, Morag Gillies, went lambing.
4 Where DP learnt to distil whisky.
5 Where the barley came from.
6 The major town in Lochaber.
7 The gorge where the cattle drovers were caught
   in the avalanche.
8 Scene of the massacre of Glencoe.
— Railway line

Skye

Canna⁴

Eigg

Tiree⁵

Mallaig
Arisaig
Ardnish
Glenuig
Roshven¹
Castle Tioram²
Meoble³
Loch Nevis
Glenfinnan
Fort William⁶
▲ Ben Nèvis
Glencoe⁸

0   5   10 kilometres

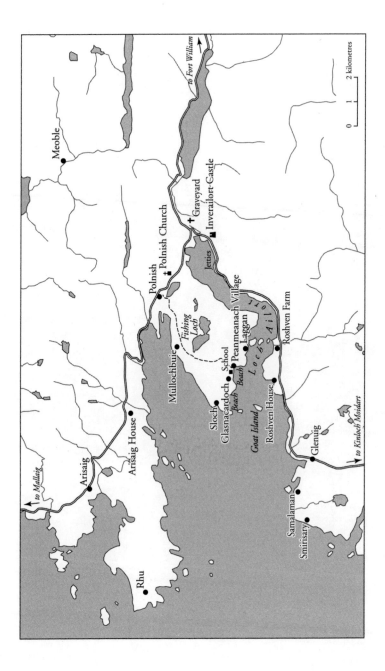

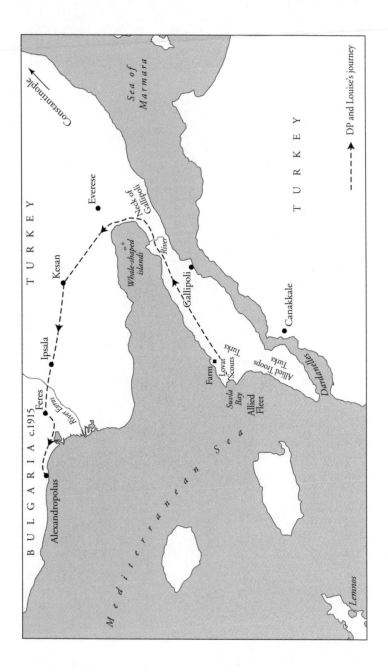

BULGARIA c.1915

T U R K E Y

T U R K E Y

Sea of
Marmara

Constantinople

Everese

Kesan

Ipsala

Feres

River Evros

Alexandropolus

Neck of
Gallipoli

Whale-shaped
islands

River

Gallipoli

Canakkale

Dardanelles

Farm

Lovat
Scouts

Turks

Suvla
Bay

Allied
Fleet

Allied Troops

Turks

Mediterranean Sea

Lemnos

- - - - ► DP and Louise's journey

Ardnish is where God was born. Anyone who has been there on a day in early May, as the sun sets over Goat Isle, would see why it is a certainty.

The peninsula is the most beautiful place on earth: the gentle hills behind the village; the towering mountains of An Stac and Roshven facing us, reflected in the sea on a calm day; the curve of the beach in front; and the islands of Eigg and Rum beyond. The clear air makes it feel as if the two islands are within reach although in fact it is a full day's rowing to get to Eigg. Ardnish was home – it is where I belong – and every day I am away I yearn to return.

Chapter 1

WAR
GALLIPOLI, OCTOBER 1915

My eyes won't open. My head is throbbing, and my wail of pain and fear brings running footsteps. There's a girl, speaking in a language similar to Gaelic. I struggle desperately to get up – one arm is useless – and I hear the words, 'You just lie there, boyo. We'll get the doctor and get some morphine inside you.'

My first spell of consciousness is agony. Flashing memories of the Turks' brutality; my helplessness and inability to move. I hear a man's voice as he takes my arm, then there's a sharp jab and a soft cool cloth caresses my sweat-drenched face. A girl's murmurings, like a lullaby, calm my anxiety, and I drift off to sleep . . .

HOME

I need to remember home; like me it is dying. My death knell is its death knell; a village that has been inhabited by my family for thousands of years is down to seven people, all of whom are over fifty. People don't visit, the fields are deteriorating and a slow unhappy decline seems inevitable.

*

I see my parents outside; my mother's knitting a pale blue woollen shawl and my father's scraping down a reed for his bagpipes. They're both laughing, and I remember why: we had two pet orphaned lambs and my brother and I were playing with them. I can picture my mother now, reaching out, drawing me to her, holding me tight.

The journey to the place where I was born – and where my heart will go when I die – begins with the puffer from Oban to Mallaig. The boat visits a host of places that were visited by Bonnie Prince Charlie in 1745, before calling at the pier in front of Inverailort Castle.

As the boat steams up Loch Ailort, a finger of land some five miles long emerges, poking into the Atlantic. On the largest of its beaches, catching all the sun, wisps of smoke from a couple of the houses draw the gaze closer still. In front of the house on the left sits an old lady on a chair – my mother.

The tide is high. The captain will run the boat up against the shore until stones scrape against the metal hull. In the next wee while, the boat will lie uncomfortably on her side as the water recedes and the crew help the passengers down a ladder and onto the seaweed-covered shore.

The boat will be met by the laird, Mr Cameron-Head, and a couple of others, no doubt. Aboard will be a friend or two coming to stay for the summer and maybe a returning local who has been away at the university or working. Calum the Post will be there to collect the mail and put some parcels on the boat to be taken away. People will materialise from all over and coal, timber, wooden boxes of food and cloth, maybe a chest of drawers or some other furniture will be lifted over the side and carried, with difficulty, to the shore.

The *craic* is good, with Mrs Cameron-Head appearing with tea for everyone, and when all is done, the crew and others head up to the inn for some food and to wait for the tide to come back in and refloat the boat. Then it will turn west and continue its voyage.

It is a two-hour walk along the ridge, with the heather-covered land sloping down to the sea on each side. There will be a stag or two, I would warrant, and certainly some cattle. A plethora of birds will fly up from their nests, luring danger away from their nesting chicks. The path peters out on the hill above the village of Peanmeanach, where there is nothing to be done but soak in the magnificence of the setting.

As the evening sun sets over the islands there is a warm glow over the crescent of houses; some just ruins now. One of the women, probably my mother, will have gone into the house to put the kettle on as she knows she has visitors.

WAR

'Now then, how are you feeling?' A cool hand touches my forehead.

'I'm thirsty. My eyes won't open. Can you help me?'

She returns with some water and props me up while I drink. Collapsing back onto the camp bed, I feel her take my hand. She bathes my sore eyes and tells me in as gentle a way as you can imagine that I have been blinded and my eyes had to be bandaged up to stop the sand getting in and to keep the flies away. She tells me my shoulder has taken a bullet, and they need to take a good look at it later, maybe on the hospital ship.

As I lie in pain, in darkness, I can hear the rustle of her clothes and smell her scent. Her murmuring voice is so reassuring and comforting. The smell of cordite, the taste of tea being held to my lips, the noise of the battle all fade into the background when she is near. I feel as if I am in my mother's arms again, and my muscles relax. The shivering subsides and the tension slips from my body as this extraordinary girl nurses me back from hell. I know she wants me to live and I am determined to do so – for her, for Louise.

As the minutes and hours tick past, the boom of the naval shelling from the shore where the engagement continues is carried up by the wind. There are a great many of us here, lying in rows in tents along the beach.

I sense I am close to death, I am in so much pain, and I need to rely on senses other than eyesight. I pray to God that I will get better and that Louise and I will go to Ardnish and home.

As dawn breaks, I listen to the groans of the injured and the agitated sounds of the nurses and medics moving wounded soldiers in and dead bodies out. We are given bread and strong coffee that makes us wince. The coffee has an unusual taste, but I am growing to like it. After the freezing cold of the night, the heat of the day penetrates the tents and I lie helpless, raking my hand back and forth on the sand.

HOME

My parents, Donald John and Morag Gillies, are the glue of the village. They are involved in everything. If they were to leave, so would everyone else. But they won't.

Then there is the old woman – or *cailleach* in the Gaelic – Eilidh Cameron. She must be about eighty, though she wouldn't know for sure herself. Her husband never returned from the army when she was young and she never met anyone else. The whaler, because he was one once, is John Macdonald, and he and his wife Aggie are in their sixties. Quiet, gentle people. Their daughters emigrated to Australia some years ago and they haven't seen them since. There is Mairi Ferguson, Sandy's mother and great friend of my mother, and Johnny 'the Bochan', a bachelor who lives for his collie dogs. He must be in his seventies now. He has a house at Peanmeanach but prefers to stay in a bothy at Sloch at the west of the peninsula. The postie, in the smart new post office house, is John MacEachan, a local man, and handy at fixing anything at all.

Mairi is a character like my mother, full of energy and go. Always a smile on her face, even when washing clothes in the burn in driving rain. Short and stocky, she's permanently dressed from head to foot in tweed woven by herself, with a grey shawl over her shoulders, even on the hottest August day. She is a kindly woman who collects wood or peat for the old, and when someone is feeling poorly she'd have a poultice or herbal remedy made up to help them.

I recall the wee wood about two hundred yards behind the village, not far off the path that takes you to the mainland. Whenever other children were around, Sandy and I would drag them off to our den by the burn in the wood. There was an oak with branches hanging over the burn with an excellent tree house that my father had helped build when we were wee, just as his father had done for him on the same branches thirty years before. The moss underneath was so deep that it came up to your ankles and was excellent for using as ammunition, and we had an old plough that we had dragged in, to use as a barricade. Often, whenever our mothers wanted to find a pan, or my father a tool, this is where they would come and look first.

We didn't learn for many years that my father was able to keep an eye on us by taking his old stalker's telescope from behind the door, steadying it against the corner of the house and observing exactly what we were up to. So when we had promised to do our schoolwork in the tree house he knew with certainty that we were building a dam instead.

WAR

As I lie here my hand can reach down to touch the drones of the bagpipes that I know so well. If I die, will they be taken back to my family? Or buried beside me? I would like somebody to take them home. Maybe my commanding officer would; he knows how famous these pipes are. When Louise comes to my bed I tell her these pipes are important to the Highlands, would she get a message to Colonel Macdonald to ask him if he could get them back to my father?

'No, DP. You'll be carrying them back yourself and playing a tune as you do so,' she replied, giving my shoulder a squeeze. This was typical of Louise. Although I couldn't see her smile, I could sense it.

Our family are the hereditary pipers to the Chieftains of the Macdonalds of Clanranald, with the bagpipes not so much an instrument of pleasure as a way of life. As I grew up it often seemed as though the sound of the chanter or the pipes themselves would fill the air, rebounding from the hills around the village. It was said that the Blackburns decided to build the great house of Roshven when they heard the pipers of Peanmeanach playing across the water after anchoring their yacht in the bay.

These very pipes were played when Prince Charlie landed at Glenfinnan in 1745. They served with the 79th in Balaclava during the Crimean war and were in my father's hands when my regiment, the Lovat Scouts, was raised to fight the Boers in South Africa in 1901. At least two of my ancestors were killed playing them, including my great-grandfather who was hacked to death with knives during the Indian mutiny. It seems I may well be the third.

'Donald Peter?' Louise's voice. 'The doctor's here to look at you.'

To look at me. That's all he does, really.

'Am I beyond saving?' I ask him.

He takes the bandage off my shoulder and mutters as he probes with his fingers, prising my glued eyes open. It hurts me, and I twist away from him and cry out.

I hear a gasp from Louise. 'Doctor Sheridan, the patient is in real pain!'

There is a silence. I can feel the tension between the two of them.

'And how do you feel today?' he asks me distractedly.

I feel a stethoscope against my chest. 'The same, I think.'

'It won't be long before we have you on the hospital ship and back to Malta.'

'Thank you, Doctor,' I say, though I can hear that he has already hurried on. Louise goes, too, but not before giving my hand a reassuring pat.

We injured are in a field station, tucked under a cliff where the Turks cannot shell us. There are maybe a hundred of us here, I am told, waiting until we get word that there is space on a hospital ship for us. The *Gloucester Castle* has taken a run to Malta with the last cargo of wounded and is due back in a week, we are told. So we wait.

Every now and again someone slips away and the Turkish prisoners come and carry him out for burial. Like all my people, I am a Roman Catholic and I worry about not having a priest to hear my last confession, and being buried amongst non-believers. I hear that there is a priest amongst the injured but that he has a head wound and cannot talk or move. I would like to have him near me as I go.

I look forward to the long sleepless nights, when Louise comes to talk. I do feel spoilt. I monopolise her time, I'm demanding, and when she is nearby I can usually find an excuse to call her over. It usually works. I know I get much more attention than the other men. I am selfish, though, and a couple of times she has put me in my place.

One day had been particularly busy, with lots of casualties arriving.

'Nurse, nurse,' I had called out as I heard her pass, 'would you help me sit up a bit?'

She did, but said firmly, 'DP, we've been working flat out for fifteen hours. There are thirty men I need to look after urgently, and you're not one of them today.'

An hour later, she came by with a bottle of water. 'Have a sip, DP, and get some sleep. I'm off to get some rest myself.'

My heart lifted again. I'd been forgiven.

Tonight, though, things are quiet. Louise is on duty and comes to sit on my cot beside me. She is all mine. We talk about the scarce water supplies and how the hospital ships would be back from Malta with space for us injured.

'But tell me how you came to be here,' Louise says, her hand on my arm.

'Louise, you won't want to hear. It's not exciting. My family lead a quiet life. It's just us and a few others tucked away in the Highlands with our animals. I'll bet you've had a much more interesting life with parties and everything.'

'Not at all. Tell me about your life, DP. I want to know about your parents, your house and your animals.'

We have the time; there is no gunfire, and dawn is a long way off. I lie in silence with only the murmur of the waves a few feet from the tent. I can hear Louise breathing as she sits patiently, knowing I'm going to talk. I know that if I stretch out my hand it will touch her.

HOME

I am only twenty-one, although I have seen as much of the Great War as anyone. My brother had just been ordained as a priest, and he and I signed up in 1914; opting for the Scouts, of course.

Although only a year, it seems a lifetime ago that Colonel Willie MacDonald walked into Ardnish and declared that I was to join him to fight the Bosche. I was just back from two years on Canna and had no plans. To take the King's shilling was the obvious thing to do; it was a tradition in the family.

The Colonel and my father had served together thirteen years before against the Boers in South Africa, and we knew, when war broke out, that we would join him; it was unthinkable that we would do otherwise. The Colonel's brother, Father Andrew, was a monk at Fort Augustus Abbey and knew my family well; he came to stay with my father from time to time and loved to go and fish in the hill lochs above the village.

The Lovat Scouts had a great Boer War and were praised by everyone. The Highland men's ability to spy the ground and report on troop movements saved countless lives. My father was proud of what they had achieved and valued highly the friendships he forged at that time.

I tell Louise that my father has a wooden leg, and she asks me how it happened . . .

*

Camped up overnight in South Africa, the Boers attacked in the darkness, filling the officers' tent with a fusillade of fire before turning on the troops and horse lines. The commanding officer, Colonel Murray, ordered an immediate bayonet charge before himself being killed. There was chaos. Many men were killed as they fled to the safety of the other Lovat Scout camp nearby. My father, however, lay in the darkness with a bullet in his thigh thinking his time was up, as the Boers celebrated wildly all around.

But then, at first light, Lord Lovat led a horse-mounted charge, and the Boers were routed.

By the time they got my father onto a ship, gangrene had set in, and so they took off the leg above the knee. He is now back at home – grateful for the War Office pension and the fact that he can still pipe. He can still ride a garron and hobble around the place on his false leg; in fact there is precious little he cannot do around the village. In some ways, he thinks it's a blessing; they have plenty of money to buy what they need, and even if he had two sound legs he wouldn't earn as much by a long shot on Ardnish.

*

'And your brother?' Louise prompts.

'Father Angus is the divisional padre. He's been sent off to the Western Front and I haven't seen him for a year. I get the occasional letter but most of the factual information has been censored. I'd love to see him again and I hope he's all right.

'He's small like our mother, with much of her about him. He's quite serious, has a very strong understanding of what is right and wrong, and God help you if you cross him. I remember him catching me baiting a cat when I was about six, and he came at me so fast I didn't know which way to turn. His fist hit me like a battering ram and I got a broken nose that's still squint and no sympathy from our mother who I ran to.'

'A priest in the family.' I can tell Louise is impressed. 'What's that like?' She shifts a bit, and I can feel her warmth against me. My pulse quickens.

'I'll tell you about him. I think you'd like him . . .'

*

The last great celebration in the village was when he was ordained. It happened in Glasgow, where we all went for a couple of days on the train.

There were about forty young men all joining the priest-hood on the same day, to be ordained by the Archbishop of Glasgow.

We were all in our finery. Father was wearing the beautiful kilt he was given by Clanranald, a long white horsehair spor-ran, the piper's tartan plaid draped over his shoulder, his dirk hanging from his waist and the elegant Glengarry hat. There is not a head that doesn't turn when he is in this kit. Mother had on a purple heather-coloured skirt that she had woven herself and Sir Arthur Astley-Nicholson, the laird of Arisaig estate, had had made into a skirt for her, and a mantilla, with her beautiful red hair almost glowing through it.

I was wearing a kilt that used to be Angus's and was far too big for me. It was the first time I'd dressed up like this; my hair was smoothed down with Brylcreem, and my woollen stockings were scratchy in the heavy army shoes that my mother had borrowed for me. I was a terribly self-conscious fifteen-year-old.

Along with all the other families we were in a quiver of excitement, and fiercely proud of our priest-to-be. Most of them came from the Isles and Lochaber – the mainstay of Catholics in Scotland, or so I'd heard.

We stayed with Aunt Aggy, my Dad's sister, and other friends and relations who had moved down to live in the big city. They all lived in tenements, on top of each other in wee rooms, sometimes two to a mattress – and toilets just a bucket in the corner. There was another family who had been great friends of my parents from Arisaig and had moved to the city a couple of years ago to find work. Cameron, the father, and his son Iain both worked in the Govan shipyards building battleships for the Royal Navy. And Aunt Aggy had a job as a cleaner in the Grand Central Hotel. They were much better off now, with enough money to be able to eat, and they were hoping to get a flat to themselves soon, in a better part of town.

It all seemed very rough to us, but they treated us like royalty and there was a tremendous party in a bar before the big day. We all went to the Barra Head, a pub frequented by those from the west and run by the redoubtable Mrs MacNeil who, it was said, had owned the place since Adam was a boy.

There was no nonsense about Protestants taking us on here, unlike in many parts of Glasgow where Catholics were given a hiding. The Catholics had been pouring into Glasgow from all over the West Highlands seeking work, and the locals feared for their jobs. The Irish, too, had come to Glasgow to seek work in the mighty industrial powerhouse that the city was. Old Mrs MacNeil didn't hesitate to come bolting out from behind the bar with her shinty stick, cracking heads left, right and centre, if people got out of order.

Although there were drams a-plenty that night, Mother was keeping everyone under control – no one would have a hangover for Angus's big day. Sandy and me she watched in particular. We had not seen much more than the odd dram before, and we were keen to live it up a bit.

The cathedral was packed with a thousand souls, we guessed. The whispering up and down the aisles was mainly in Gaelic; you could hear the soft lilt of Barra and Eriskay. My father said that were three men being made priests from the village of Invergarry alone. Here and there was the unmistakeable broad tone of Glasgow Scots.

The choir sang and we competed with them, nearly lifting the roof off. As you can imagine for a lad used to no more than fifty in our wee church at Polnish, it was quite the thing.

In came the procession: a dozen altar boys, then the same number of priests and, lastly, Archbishop Maguire wearing his tall mitre and carrying his crozier. The singing rose and fell, and the men were welcomed into the priesthood. A circle of hair about four inches across was shaved from each of their heads, which my sister Sheena told me was called a 'tonsure'.

Angus came and joined us before the service for a few moments. There was much hugging and kissing, shaking of hands, and then he was off again. We would see him later, on the train. My mother was sobbing like a baby. Our family had always been emotional; it was my mother who'd got that going, she couldn't be doing with all that formality. I would wrestle and twist away as she clasped me to her at any time, even when my friends were watching.

After two hours, we were done, and there was a rush for the 4.10 train to Mallaig, so we could get home that night. MacBraynes had laid on a special steamer to take people from Glasgow to Barra and the other islands. There would be a lot of whisky and not much sleep on the boat that night.

The train was packed as we headed up north, where a huge party was planned. My brother looked funny in his new black habit. Sheena and I both felt his tonsure; as smooth as a baby's bottom, she said, to her brother's discomfort.

'Not much of a halo on you yet,' said his disrespectful sister. Mother preened and glowed as people came from all over the train to shake his hand and wish him well.

The train clattered and rocked up Loch Lomond and across Rannoch Moor. You could see the steam yacht on the loch that Sir John Maxwell had shipped up to Corrour in pieces from Glasgow by train. It was reassembled on the side of the loch and was used to ferry his guests the eight miles down to the new lodge he had built.

The spring sun made the hills glow orange and the rocky outcrops glisten like silver. The mountains of Glencoe had snow still in the gullies, and alongside the track the stags would gallop away from the train as it approached. Ben Nevis towered above us as we pulled into Fort William and many of the passengers disembarked. But just as many newcomers got on, most of whom would be joining us for the big celebration that night.

Bottles of Long John whisky were passed around as we set off for the final hour on the train, and three fiddlers – Alex Macdonald and his two brothers from Avoch – got the party off to a good start in the front carriage. They were coming to the village to provide a bit of music, having played at a wedding in the Fort the night before. Sleep was a thing that fiddlers never seemed to need. They simply curled up after the evening was finished, always the last to bed down, and were up and off to the next ceilidh the following morning.

We felt heady and excited as the train stopped especially for us at Polnish, and the procession headed off over the hill in single file towards Ardnish and home. My father was on the grey garron with his wooden leg sticking out at the side. Mother, Sheena, myself, Mairi and Sandy shot off ahead to get some fires going and water boiling before everyone else arrived.

It was all done, though. The neighbours from across the peninsula who hadn't come down to the service had been hard at work.

Those from all over Ardnish and friends and cousins had arrived, armed with bottles of whisky, haunches of meat, and bread. There must have been a hundred people present, and almost all of them, it appeared, were at pains to point out their relationship to us.

'I'm your grandfather's sister's daughter from Bohuntin,' said a white-haired *cailleach*.

'Your great-auntie Lexie had two boys, of which I am the youngest,' declared a man whose name I never caught.

The whisky was opened, savoured and complimented; the smiles became broader and laughter louder. The Auch boys were urged to get their fiddles out and then the ceilidh was in full flow. Faces grew bright red from the exertions and the alcohol, and clothes were shed as the May warmth was exacerbated by the sheer number of us cramped in the front room. Children danced with grand-parents, teenage boys tried to unbalance the girls as they spun round the room, and not a single person sat on the sidelines.

My father, Father Angus and myself played eightsomes on the pipes; it would probably be the last time we would all play together, what with my brother heading off to the church.

My father was a doer, rather than a talker. My mother's genes, on the other hand, had been inherited by Sheena, so without much persuasion she was up making a speech.

'My goodness, isn't the church lucky to have got Angus? There isn't a girl in Lochaber who wouldn't have him in a trice! I hope they care for him . . .'

And so on. There was much shushing from our brother and whoops from the audience as she recounted how his determination to join the clergy had been given a serious wobble when that brazen young hussy Maggie Wilson came up to stay with the Macphersons two or three years ago.

Anyway, her speech was well received, and after Angus stood up and said a few words of thanks to everyone, the party really buckled down into something quite serious.

Every stick of furniture had been removed from the croft house and still there wasn't an inch of space. Food was handed out to a big table outside, while indoors, haunches of venison and mutton, piles of steaming potatoes and cabbage, and a big stack of herring rolled in oats lay beside a big salmon that had been caught on the Ailort in the nets only the day before and donated to the celebrations by the estate. Little did they know, but the rest of the fare probably came from their ground, too, not that anyone would have said anything.

The dance now was the Highland Schottische, where Jimmy and Hazel Macdonald always showed the way. And, with the exuberance and giddy excitement always encouraged by whisky and dancing, romance was in the air. Girls would be twirled off their feet and the lads would relish the chance to hold them tight. From time to time, a stealthy couple would slip off towards the cattle shed, always noticed by the grandparents sitting in benches along the wall.

As the evening wore on, the moon came out and bathed the shore with a light you could see to read by. My brother and I walked along the beach, talking as dawn broke; both of us were aware that it would never be the same again: us, the village, and the gathering of friends and kin like the night just gone.

'What will you do for a job, Donald Peter?' Angus asked.

I talked about getting a fishing boat; fishermen never starve.

'There will always be plenty of fish around these waters,' I said. 'But I might join the army for a few years. I'll know in a couple of years when I have finished my schooling. Mother wants me to go to university, to better myself, to move away.'

I sighed. 'I'll never be away from Ardnish for long, Angus, I'll promise you that. Father says I should go and help out old Tearlach Maclean, our mother's cousin on Canna. There is great demand for his whisky since Lloyd George put his tax up to fifteen shillings a gallon. He's in his seventies now and is finding it difficult to manage.'

'Aye, but it'll be lonely for you, DP,' said Angus.

'I might just do it, though. It'll be fun getting one over the excise men. Those Mackinnon girls on the island are easy on the eye too,' I said, giving him a playful punch on the arm.

The hooded crows were cawing as they wheeled above us in the early morning. Gulls floated on the sea, and a seal poked its head up amongst them to survey the debris of the party. The village was full, with comatose bodies lying on the floor in every house. The whisky would surely help them sleep despite the hardness of the floor and the lack of a blanket or mattress.

I was sweet on a lass called Kirsty McAlistair from Glenuig at the time. Kirsty and I had danced like mad March hares; there was hardly a reel we'd missed apart from when I had had a spin with my mother, and Sandy's, too. I felt the heat from Kirsty's body through her cotton dress, but although I yearned to kiss her, I never had the chance.

That night, I pushed her boat off the beach and watched the McAlistairs row, unsteadily, the three miles across to their house. It was the last time I saw her. Her father worked for the estate, but it had laid him off, and the family moved to Glasgow shortly after.

WAR

Louise is silent for a long time. I wonder if my storytelling has sent her to sleep, but I feel her hand touch my arm.

'Did you ever get that fishing boat?' she whispers.

'Not yet, maybe I will yet, though,' I say, although with my injuries we both know it is unlikely. 'I went off to Canna for a couple of years to help Tearlach make whisky. It would take a bit of time to tell you about it, Louise, but I think you'd enjoy the story. It was illegal whisky, we were on an island, and we spent our time avoiding the Customs and Excise men. I'm tired now, so I'll tell you another time if that's all right.'

'Of course, DP. I won't let you forget ... You're not coarse like many of the other soldiers, DP. You know things, too. You're an educated man.'

'No, no. I'm not, I'm not,' I insist. 'But we did have a strict upbringing – no swearing in the house. My father treated my mother well, they respect each other, and there has always been a feeling that God is somewhere nearby. Grace before every meal and family prayers on our knees before bed. My parents were always teaching us things.'

'Mmm,' murmurs Louise. 'It wasn't like that in our house. Rest now, and I'll be back to see you later.'

As she heads off, the patients come to life with groans and coughs. I can hear a man peeing into a glass jar. There are raised voices as a soldier is brought down from the lines, probably with dysentery. Gulls screech; plenty of pickings for them. I had heard that losing one of the senses made the others more alert, and I am aware of straining to hear and identify everything much more than I did before.

Outside, I hear female Turkish voices. There are a couple of women who come along the shore and sell cigarettes, coffee, bread and other things to the soldiers. They do a roaring trade, with troops queuing to buy everything. The women take anything as currency: army boots, pound notes and even the contents of our ration packs. The officers did their best at first to stop it, but the women would just appear somewhere else, and there was always a willing buyer. The officers are concerned that our secrets will get back to the Turks, as no doubt they do, but it seems to us that our shortage of water and the position of the casualty station are the only two things they have learned, which they were certain to know, anyway.

The men revel in having Turkish cigarettes, which are much stronger than those issued to us and rather more exotic.

Louise has a close friend, and when I had been in the clearing station for a few days she bought her over.

'DP, this is Prissie, my best friend. She's working with the doctors in the operating tent.'

Now and again, Prissie comes by and we have a wee chat; she is very amusing and I am delighted to listen to her.

One day, she appeared with some dried green beans, which she'd bought from the Turkish women and had cooked.

She passed them around the tent. 'Eat these,' she encouraged the men, 'they're good for you.'

Not many vegetables come our way so we're happy to comply.

Chapter 2

WAR

Louise is coming. I can hear her footsteps.

It must be late; there is only the snuffling from the man beside me. Beyond I hear the rhythmic crash of the waves on the rocky beach and the accompanying rumble of the stones as they shift with the water. An occasional rifle shot can be heard on the hills above – maybe some poor woman is a widow now.

Louise kneels beside the bed and takes my hand. 'The sergeant's just died.'

We don't talk for a while. I think about him. He'd been shot in the thigh and had lost a lot of blood. His strong Lancashire accent was but a whisper, and although he must have been in terrible pain, he suffered it silently. More than half of those who make it as far as the field hospital end up dying – a limb blown off or a bullet hole, often in the head as that's what the Turkish snipers can see sticking above the trench. When a big push happens, huge numbers of men spill in here. There are separate tents for those with dysentery, the most common ailment.

Louise clearly enjoys my stories and I look forward to our conversations.

As the days pass, I lie there and remind myself of things to tell her. Without the distractions of sight, I seem to possess an extraordinary ability to recollect the smallest things.

*

I remember an incident from almost ten years ago. Sheena and I were walking along Loch Eilt on the way home from spending a few days in Glenfinnan with friends of the family. Along came Mr Cameron-Head in his new car. It was the first car I'd seen, and we stepped out of the way to let him pass. My mouth was wide with wonder, apparently, and I was stuck for words when he stopped and offered us a lift.

He talked all the way home. 'Real leather seats. It's American,' he said, 'a Cadillac. They're the best.'

Sheena wasn't struck dumb like me and blethered away to him quite happily.

He offered her a cigarette – her first, she said unnecessarily, as she coughed and spluttered.

There isn't a detail too small for me to remember of that day: how small the rough track was for that big car, how I had to get out and push stones out of the way, and how grown-up my sister was after all.

*

Louise hates Doctor Sheridan, and therefore so do I. Every time he comes to the tent there is tension; she lets nothing slip and he knows it.

She challenges him constantly. 'And where did you train? Did you know Matron Murray at St Bart's? Who was there? What do you think about this man's fever?'

He gets his revenge, I suspect, by prodding and poking me a lot more harshly than he needs to. Being treated by him is like being wounded all over again, rather than the silky healing caress of Louise.

I can tell he wants to get away from us as quickly as possible, so thankfully his visits are short. Lots of other tents to visit, he exclaims as he departs.

Louise is from Wales, and over time I learn about her family: her father's hell in the coal mines and how it is her dream to be a farmer's wife.

I determine there and then that I will be that farmer if I am to survive – although making a living in the village is barely possible. So I tell her I will go home to be a fisherman and have my own boat, or else be a ghillie for the Astley-Nicholsons at Arisaig House. We don't discuss the likelihood of my making it back alive at all.

Every day, one of the nurses, usually Louise, takes off my bandage and cleans my eyes with some vinegar. It stings like hell, as it involves opening my eyelids. Today, I think for the first time that maybe I can see light with my right eye, but my eyelids don't want to stay open and I cast the thought from my mind. The doctors tell me nothing, though it's clear that my shoulder is well on the mend. I had big blisters on my face from the scalding water, but they have hardened and the scabs are coming off. Not a pretty sight, I know.

Although I talk to Louise about fishing or being a ghillie,

we both know that with my ruined eyesight there is little chance of either. I take some comfort in thinking I could teach the pipes, like my father, and there should be an invalid pension, too.

Louise has a dog at home, which she loves. She hopes her little brother is looking after it. It's a sheepdog called Daffie, which she rescued when it was the size of half a pound of butter. The neighbours had despaired of finding a taker for it, and the puppy would have been drowned had Louise not claimed him for her own.

*

'It's getting light,' Louise says. 'I have to get things ready for breakfast. I hope there's enough food for all the men. We need supplies soon.'

Thinking of her, I drift off into a fitful sleep. What do people mean when they talk about falling in love? Is it constant thought about the girl, the wish to touch her all the time, the feeling of abandonment when they move on, or you feel you are being ignored? It's not about marriage or children; it's more immediate and personal than that. It's deep inside. It's raw and omnipresent.

Thinking about Louise drowns out the pain. All my contact with her is soothing, caring, considerate. I wonder what she thinks of me. She makes me feel special – would she do all that she does for me if I wasn't special? The question tortures my every waking hour.

It is a problem: the nurses have had it drummed into them that getting emotionally attached to a patient is a disaster. He may be married, or he will get better and leave.

Or even worse, he will die. In my case, I'm an unattractive redhead with two very serious injuries. I may not die now, but I will be disabled for life. Not the sort of person who would win her heart.

Nevertheless, I yearn to tell her that she is the one for me and that we will run off together, that the hours are painful without her, and that when I sense her pass by without stopping, my heart lurches. I want her to sit beside me and tell me more of her life. But if she shows me any affection, I'm scared that my feelings will all spill out and everything will be ruined, that she will be posted elsewhere.

'Bottle it up,' I tell myself again and again. 'Say nothing.'

I have fallen in love with her though, there is no doubt of that.

*

Can it only be four months ago that we embarked? It had gone from summer in England to the heat of Egypt to the freezing wet winter of Turkey. The Lovat Scouts saw 1,200 of the best Highland men – young, eager, the pick of their villages – now reduced to half that number. The ones I come across in the tent are often about to die. They come from Applecross and Beauly, from Uist to Skye. Their communities will suffer greatly by the wiping out of their young men. The cities are cushioned – incomers will soon fill the houses or take the jobs. But in the Highlands, like my own Ardnish, the death of only two or three young men would result in a huge area becoming unpopulated within a generation.

The war in Gallipoli had been going badly. General Hamilton wanted more troops. We had been expecting to go to the Western Front, but we all agreed that Turkey sounded better. In early August 1915, two regiments of us Lovat Scouts were loaded onto a ship called RMS *Andania* at Devonport.

The mood amongst the men was high. We enjoyed the summer sun on deck, playing cards, eating well and enduring the endless exercises the sergeants put us through. Three weeks later, we were in Malta for refuelling and to take on supplies, when we discovered that the ship alongside had many injured from the Scottish Horse regiment. Several of our men went across and talked to them. Our boys were shocked by what they heard: pointless attack after pointless attack trying to gain precious ground, with Turkish machine-gunners placed at the top of the hills with unrestricted views down onto our position. Of the 700 in the regiment, two thirds would get killed or injured in a single push. And the lack of water was critical. These men had been fighting in 100 degrees with no clean water; they said that while the injured were lying on the beach, waiting to be collected, they would go across to the water pipes from the ships and pierce them with their knives just to get a drop. These stories sobered us up a bit.

One day the Scottish Horse called for some piping, so myself and another went on deck and played a few jigs and reels to cheer everyone up. It clearly didn't get everyone's approval – one English officer told us to shut up or he'd put us in chains!

From there we travelled to Alexandria in Egypt where we stayed for a week. This included a forced march for a day and a night to 'give the boys some exercise'. We also had some shore leave, and Sandy, myself and three others from our platoon found some bars and a nightclub to enjoy. It was bewildering and exciting for me. There were men from all over the world – in turbans and Aussie hats, Foreign Office men in crisp white shorts, Africans and Indians, officers and privates – jostling at the bar, with the good-natured shrieks and shouts of soldiers on a night out. Voluptuous women would sit on our knee, encouraging us to smoke a hookah and buy them a drink, only to float off the minute they had it in their hand. We would dance until long after daybreak and then stagger back to our lines, giggling at everything and anything.

In Egypt we had unloaded our ponies, shaggy Highland beasts more used to the cold moorland of Wester Ross than the dry heat of an Egyptian summer. When we signed up for the regiment, we were paid more if we bought our own mounts with us – many of them had been carrying the Scouts' children on their backs just a few months before.

Now loaded onto two smaller ships, the SS *Sarnia* and SS *Abasseieh*, we set off again and, after a brief stop on the Greek island of Lemnos, we finally arrived off Gallipoli on 26 September. The sight as we arrived was extraordinary: dozens of ships were at anchor. The hospital ships, the *Gloucester Castle* and the *Essequibo*, were lit up with bulbs and had red crosses painted on their sides. Our battleships were pounding the hills, and little boats were scurrying back and forth, taking ammunition and food onto the beach and returning with injured men.

We were moored opposite Suvla Bay, the northerly point of the invasion. The Australians and New Zealanders were at the southerly tip fifteen miles away, with other troops spread in between. Most of our boys stood watching on the deck as we steamed in, a knot of fear in even the bravest man's stomach.

We sat at anchor for half a day, waiting for the order to disembark, and as darkness fell we were loaded into covered boats called 'beetles' to take us onshore. The beetles were new. When the landings first took place months ago, the men sat exposed in open lighters, offering the Turks the opportunity to direct their fire straight into the boats as they landed on the beach. In many cases, not a single man made it onto the sand alive, and the boats would float back and forth full of rotting corpses in the heat of the summer.

*

There is some excitement in the tent. A hospital ship has returned from Malta and casualties are being chosen to go out to it. The most seriously injured take priority.

Louise comes along. 'We're putting some injured on the ship, DP, but I'm afraid it won't include you. I'm so sorry.'

An officer is directing stretcher bearers. 'Take him . . . and him. Be careful with him. He's got a broken back.'

Within a day, the tent is full again.

*

The first week after we landed we were on fatigues, taking water bowsers up to the front, putting up tents, carrying stores and so on. There was one huge advantage: we could swim in the sea. Everyone did and without a stitch of clothing.

One sharp-witted lad shouted, 'Sir, if we get a mirror we can reflect the glare off Gillies and blind the Turks!' True enough, there can be few whiter people than a red-haired Highland lad on his first trip to a foreign country. I blushed, only adding to the effect.

Colonel Willie Macdonald was our Commanding Officer, and I was his batman and piper. He set up a crack company of snipers to which I was seconded.

Ever since I'd signed up I'd noticed that the other regiments think us odd, travelling as we do on Highland ponies, telescopes around our shoulders. And there's the curious, familiar relationship between us and our officers, which is in stark contrast to the extremely formal relationship of the officers and guardsmen of the English regiments.

Like the rest of our officers, Colonel Willie is one of the lairds, and is the owner of the Long John whisky distilleries in Fort William. He and I get along famously, and he is always keen to know how my father is faring. Although I spent almost two years with old Tearlach Maclean on Canna distilling illegal whisky I never told the Colonel about it, but he knows I know a lot about whisky.

He was at Peanmeanach when I got back from Canna a year or more ago; there for some fishing with his brother. He'd arrived while my father and I were out, and was having tea with my mother. The table was covered in drawings of a spirit receiver that Tearlach was keen to have. He raised his eyebrow at me when I came in and scrambled to collect the papers together, blushing the same red as my hair.

Us snipers would, on occasion, lie in some scrub for days on end, often within yards of the enemy, waiting to get a shot at an important officer. Being stalkers, which most of the Scouts were, we had a real familiarity with a rifle and a 250-yard shot was quite feasible, as my friend Sandy was to demonstrate before too long.

From early October the regiment was moved into the forward trenches. The men we replaced looked haggard and exhausted. Many were wounded. Despite this, there was a bit of banter and some helpful words as we moved into their positions: 'Don't put your head past here, and don't go further along than that bush . . .'

They were full of good advice. In the three weeks that they had been here there had been a major push by our troops to take the hilltops, yet despite huge losses on each side, not an inch of ground had been gained and the men were in a desperate state.

Within a week we, too, were in a similarly bad way. The rotten food, the water (when there was any) that tasted of decaying meat, and the relentless spells of heavy freezing rain all took their toll. Bodies were everywhere: our own and the Turks. Many were just out of reach, and an attempt to reach them and take them off for a burial would result in a shot being fired. It was just far too dangerous.

There had been a couple of armistices over the summer where troops from both sides dug communal pits and exchanged cigarettes with the enemy. The Turks often burned their dead, causing an even worse stench and making us retch for days. In one trench, a hand stuck out of the bank and men shook it as they passed by. I couldn't even look at it.

Many men had severe dysentery. The smell, the excruciating embarrassment and discomfort. Quickly, terrible sores became the norm. A couple of times there was an extraordinary downpour, with inches of rain or snow falling in two hours.

Our trenches were flooded, and we were pretty sure that the water that poured down the hillside came from evacuated Turkish positions beyond us. There was no medicine that made any difference, and at one stage in early November, seventy per cent of our troops had to be pulled off the front line. Rations were infrequent and pretty dire.

Sandy and I were fine, however; we gobbled down any food that came our way. Sandy would chuckle, 'It's just like my mother's cooking. If you can survive hers, then you can survive anything.'

There was the odd laugh, as often occurs in times of crisis. Captain Kenny Macdonald from Skye was the duty medical officer, and as the number 9 pill for diarrhoea had long since run out, he would issue numbers 7 and 2, or 5 and 4 instead.

I recall an English soldier saying, with admiration in his voice, 'If there were any soldiers in the world who could enjoy the terrible rain and freezing cold, it would be the Lovat Scouts.' It was a strange comfort.

One night a Turkish patrol blundered into our line by mistake and was captured. I never saw them myself, but apparently they, too, were in an awful state. They were sent down to an enclosure on the beach for questioning. A plan had been hatched that the prisoners would be well treated and allowed to escape in the hope that they would go back and encourage others to surrender. And so a Turkish work party was sent off, unguarded, to collect firewood, but at the end of the day they dutifully returned, laden with mountains of wood. They knew where they were better off. We heard that a lot of prisoners on both sides had been shot as soon as they were captured at the early stage of the campaign.

The battle was really about sniping, with sharpshooters from both sides trying to take each other out. Sometimes, even in the relative safety of a trench, a couple of our men would be shot and it would take several days to identify where the Turkish sniper was or, more usually, where he had been.

The Turkish prisoners told us about one of their snipers, who was nicknamed 'Percy' for some forgotten reason, who had a tremendous hit rate on our men. Because of him, during the month of November we lost many men.

Angus McKay, an experienced deer stalker from Strathnaver, became obsessed with getting this sniper, and forged a plan. He made himself an entire suit of clothes with grasses stitched in, and darkened his face and hands with creosote he'd got from the store. He then wound a khaki bandage around his head, sprouting grass and twigs. We heard that a sergeant jumped out of his skin when he rested his tea on a knoll, and the knoll moved off.

McKay headed off alone one night to get into a position that had a clear view over their lines. He took only a wet rag to suck and no food. No mosquito would make him flinch, he told us. We all agreed he must be hardened by the ferocious midges of Helmsdale.

Anyway, a week passed and he still hadn't returned. We assumed he must have been captured or shot. But then, one morning, he was back. Terribly skinny, with eyes staring out of a blackened, hollow face. McKay had been lying in a gulley a hundred yards behind our lines, maybe two hundred from the Turks, having identified a bit of brush where he thought a man could hide. He watched and watched that bit of brush, and finally shot Percy, just before the fellow could shoot him. McKay was celebrated up and down the lines. The deciding factor for him, he explained, was that no bird would sit on the branches of the bush – they always veered off at the last moment.

Apparently, when the campaign began there was very poor medical cover, with only two doctors for the 100,000 British troops. The huge losses meant that many injured were lying covered in blood and sand in rows along the beach in the blistering heat of the summer for days, waiting for attention. When they were ferried out to the hospital ships they would often not be allowed on as they were full.

But in the last few months, things got better, when the Queen Alexandra nurses set up tented medical stations on the beaches.

One day, in the trenches, I was sitting trying to get a nail that was coming through the heel of my boot when one of our planes flew over. It circled a bit and was clearly in trouble; you could hear the engine stuttering. All the Brits were watching, and the Turks, too. As it came in to land on the dried-out salt lake, one of its wheels collapsed and it toppled over. The pilots leaped out and scampered off, which was just as well, as the Turks, just for the hell of it, immediately began to use it for target practice with their artillery. And my God, they were accurate.

HOME

Louise is asking me about my boyhood friend, Sandy . . .

I haven't said much about him yet. He and I were only a year apart in age and had been brought up side by side in Peanmeanach. We were the only two of our age, his mother Mairi and mine were sound friends, and I can't remember ever being apart from him. We were twins, in a way.

His father was away at the fishing for weeks at a time, in Mallaig or Ullapool, following the herring. It was hard work. The boats would be offshore, even throughout the winter, with no shelter from the worst of the weather. They would come in laden with their catch, which would be unloaded onto the shore, where women would gut and salt the fish before stacking them in barrels and sending them off to the cities.

Sandy and I often played on the beach in front of the house, fetched water from the spring for the old folk in the village, and had a good time together, always outside. Even in the rain Sandy's mother would chase us out with the word '*Machashaw!*' Get out of here!

Three days a week, a teacher would come across from

Arisaig and teach us in the smartest building. The school board built it at about the time I was born. Well, the school board paid for it; it was our fathers who built it. It had cut stone, rather than the round field stone that all our croft houses were built from, and a slate roof rather than heather thatch. Two rooms: one of which the teacher lived in, then the school room. There was a privy out the back, with running water. We had nothing so smart at our house.

There were four of us pupils, from all over Ardnish. We took a piece of lunch with us and a bottle of milk if we were lucky, and in the winter we had to bring an armful of wood or peat for the stove. All classes were in English, and we were forbidden to speak the Gaelic. Learning Latin from English, when we didn't speak either, wasn't that easy.

Mr Erskine, our teacher who hailed from Glasgow, seemed to be no more than a boy himself, but he worked us hard, and we were in a good position by the time we were fourteen and ready to go to work. Or sixteen, as I was; my mother made me stay on so that I could go to university if the opportunity arose.

The school building was by the sea, and I remember our indignation when a few days after Mr Erskine started at the school he turned the room around so that we couldn't look out of the window at the sea. Sandy, always the daring one, turned it back again the following weekend. Mr Erskine gave him six of the best with his trousers down, which our mothers agreed was thoroughly deserved.

Mairi, or Aunt Mairi as we called her when we were young, was a great maker of tweed. Being from the

Hebridean island of Eriskay, she had learned the craft from her parents and had got everyone in Peanmeanach into making it. The spring was the collecting of the crotal, the lichens which give the tweed its peculiar orange colour. The crotal was scraped off the rocks with spoons and piled into a basket. Mairi would buy about a hundred fleeces after the clipping of the sheep. She was very particular about which fleeces she chose: no black wool, and none with brambles or muck in it. Then the wool would be washed, combed, dyed and spun into a yarn. She would get everyone from the village to help tease and wash the wool, and even got them singing the waulking songs from the islands. There was an old pedal-driven loom that she worked into the small hours, just as her father and grandfather had done before her.

The Astley-Nicholsons were very taken by her distinctive orange tweed and would take as much as she could produce for the Arisaig estate tweed. It may seem an odd choice, but for eight months a year, when the first frost arrives, the grasses on the mountains turn a surprising shade of orange, so the tweed is perfect for the stalkers and their guests to approach the deer unseen.

I was delighted when Sandy joined our Company, and we had a tremendous three days' leave after our two months' training in the Scottish Borders. Armed with our sleeping kit and some fishing lines, we spent the day on a river, caught lots of fish and then went to the local pub and drank beer. Apart from a rare trip to Mallaig or Fort William we had rarely experienced a pub before. It was an establishment of which we approved greatly.

The weather was unusually lovely and we lay soaking it all in. We built a good fire every night and sat up talking about home and how we were going to go back as soon as we could. We talked about girls and what it would be like to make love. We talked about my injured father, who Sandy had seen only a short while before. I laughed when Sandy told me how cranky he was becoming and how he kept my mother running around doing errands for him. *That* wouldn't last, we agreed.

Sandy was from a family called Ferguson that had left St Kilda at the time of his grandfather. St Kilda is a series of islands sixty miles west of the Scottish mainland. The fifty or so inhabitants live a harsh life, enduring wild weather in the long hard winters. Tragically, almost all the babies died shortly after birth, but a Nurse Barclay spent time on the island and soon discovered what the problem was. She watched in horror as the islanders practised a Christian ceremony of anointing the umbilical cord with oil from the body of a fulmar bird. Nurse Barclay realised that the babies were being given tetanus and soon put a stop to it.

Sandy told me a story of a crew of four oarsmen taking five men and two boys, including an ancestor of his, in their big boat from the main island, called Hirta, to a 500-foot-tall rock, Stac an Armin, which lay four miles away. The seven of them were deposited with food and supplies for a couple of weeks. The plan was that when they had done their work they would light a grass fire and the boat would come back and fetch them.

There, Sandy's ancestor and the others used nooses on the end of long poles to snare fulmar seabirds, swiping at the birds as they flew past and catching them in nets until they had accumulated a big enough pile. The oil would be used for lighting in those days, and the feathers were sold for bedding. They also harvested guillemots, gannets and puffins by the hundreds of thousands. After two weeks they were ready to finish and get home.

Day after day, they lit the fire, and still there was no movement on the main island. They were there from September throughout the winter, putting up with 100mph winds, snow sweeping across the Atlantic, and just a small bothy for shelter, largely underground, with a stone roof sealed with turf they could just crawl into.

Imagine – no fuel for a fire and just raw seabirds to eat. Eventually, in the spring, Macleod of Macleod's factor came to collect the rent, and the men frantically waved the boat down as it passed. They got back to Village Bay on Hirta to discover that there had been a terrible dose of smallpox, and so many had died that that they hadn't been able to launch the boat.

Chapter 3

WAR

I've decided to ask Louise to describe herself. It's difficult for me to ask while pretending to be a detached observer. I hope she'll let me feel her hair and put a hand on her leg – maybe more. She bursts out laughing and says she's too short, too skinny and has boring dirty hair which needs cutting.

I yearn to know how slim she is, how her mouth moves when she smiles and what colour her eyes are. The ardour of a passionate youth is not satisfied by her self-deprecating response, so I back off to try again at a later date. Instead, we complain good-naturedly about the food, the weather and anything else which constitutes safe ground.

I doze off and wake up with a start. My body is racked with coughing and I am soaked with sweat. I shiver in the warmth. A nurse brings me brackish water and I feel miserable. I listen to the distant voices of the medical staff, hoping to hear Louise. The groans and occasional cries of pain from the injured provide a constant background tinnitus that we're becoming immune to. My eyes are sore, my shoulder is sore, and I feel so weak that I cannot even lift my head. Not a man an attractive nurse would be interested in.

I think of my mother . . .

HOME

Morag is my mother. She is a very small woman, and very powerful in that non-physical way wee people often are. She is hardy and brave and stubborn, and was said to have been a beauty in her youth, although the working in the fields, the hard days and often damp bed have given her stiff joints and a bent back. She keeps her own counsel and gets to know people well before she judges them. She will always lend people an ear and is ever a voice of reason and sense.

As the years passed she became more than just a mother to me; she became the mother to those in the village. And she stood no nonsense. It wasn't just the bairns who feared her when they stepped out of line.

Her own father was a book-keeper in Glasgow, and as she grew up she never wanted for anything. She had come on holiday with a friend from Glasgow and met my father for the first time at Arisaig House.

There was a wedding for one of the staff at the big house, and my father had gone across to play the pipes for it. My mother was a relative of the girl who was getting married and had come up for the celebration. Many people met their future spouses at weddings in those days, when travel was a rare thing.

Love must be a powerful thing, as from the day she arrived at Peanmeanach she must have known that a comfortable life was not for her. It's not that we were lacking anything because we weren't; it was just that we had a simple life. Porridge and herring were our staple diet. Tea was, like sugar, rare. She only went to Fort William once or twice a year.

My father didn't speak English to her from the day they got married. He said that she had to learn the Gaelic or she would be miserable and lonely. It might just as easily have been her choice, though, as she would surely have felt the need to learn it quickly. Many of the people in the village didn't have the English at all, and so by the time her first born arrived she could even swear in our language as well as the next person.

I try to imagine her first few weeks of married life: no talk with her husband – or anyone else for that matter – and the winter rain sweeping across the sea from the Americas, and being expected to go out with the other women, ankle deep in the sea, to collect the shellfish.

She never went back to Glasgow from the day of her wedding until the day Angus was made a priest, even though Father was abroad a lot soldiering.

I wish that she would have had more children who survived, although God knows how she would have fed them. I was born late with Angus eight years older than me and Sheena three years older than him. My parents had another three children, but the oldest one of them died aged two of pneumonia, and the other two died straight after their birth. I was the last born.

My sister Sheena was very active, never sat down for a minute. When our father was working at the building of Roshven, Sheena would go across and help out. The Blackburns had a cousin called Margaret who often came to stay at Roshven and became a good friend to my sister. It was from Margaret that Sheena learned to swim, a rare thing around there.

Sheena called Margaret 'Lady', because when they first met Sheena was very young and Margaret was a very sophisticated teenager. They used to head off together to gather shellfish: razor shells and mussels. When it was warmer they would dive for scallops and sometimes even oysters off Roshven farm, where the River Ailort flowed into the sea. We were always being given findings to eat that she had collected from the sea, whether it was seaweed or whelks. Most were horrid, but sometimes she had great success. The best of these was a huge lobster that she and Margaret caught in a pot that they set out, off Sloch. It was as long as a small child was high, and Sheena could hardly lift it. I was only ten years old at the time. Apparently, my father had to make a big fire outside, wrap it in wet leaves and bake it on a sheet of tin. Dripping in butter, it fed the dozen people of Peanmeanach, and was so rich not one of them could manage another morsel afterwards.

The sea around Ardnish has always been full of fish of all sorts. It was our staple diet, but everyone preferred meat. Meat was rare, though. Allan the whaler would have one cow, and it would have one calf a year. That cow would give them milk all year round, and then the calf would be sold in the autumn to raise money to buy provisions to last the winter. Few people ate beef; it was just too precious.

The sheep belong to the laird, as do the red deer. However, there might occasionally be a hind with a broken leg which had to be 'put out of its misery'. This always tended to occur around about Christmas, it seemed to me.

We didn't have friends of our age to play with. Sandy and I, of course, had each other, but as families had moved away Angus had no one and Sheena likewise – that's why she looked forward to Margaret's visits so much. However, very often it didn't matter how old or young people were. Fathers would play cards and tell stories to wee girls; grandmothers would reel and jig with teenage boys. In the cities it isn't the same, I'm told; old people get awfully lonely.

It was said that Mother would get a medal from the King for something she did, but she never did. It concerned the islands of St Kilda. Mother, Aggie and Mairi were down by the burn at the spot where it runs into the sea. They were doing the washing, and Mother was scrubbing Father's clothes clean of the animal blood that had soaked them. My mother had to go off to get the tea ready, and as she walked back along the beach she saw a black ball bobbing in the water a short distance offshore. As it was out of reach, she left it alone, but she returned that evening to see if it had come closer. Fishing it into her hand with a stick, she saw that it was a sheep's bladder. It had a knot tied in it, and attached to it was a tiny wooden shoe-like container. She slid it open and found a piece of paper with a message written in Gaelic on it: 'The Fulmars are diseased, we have little food left, please help. Feb 1897 St Kilda.'

There followed a frustrating time for her as she strove to get the policeman in Arisaig to do something about it. Upon failing, she turned to Sir Arthur Astley-Nicholson at the big house, but he was away, and so she walked the thirteen-mile return journey for two days in a row to try and meet with him and convince him to help. The factor was not keen to see his master bothered, but she refused to give up until the laird saw her. She sat on the front door-step for hours on end waiting for him to get home.

Sir Arthur immediately agreed to help and sent a telegram to a contact of his in the Home Office. The slow wheels of bureaucracy turned until mother eventually learned that a Navy boat had been sent from Oban.

The *Oban Times* wrote an article on its front page headed 'MORAG GILLIES OF ARDNISH SAVES 50 LIVES'. It said that an islander claimed that if the boat had not been sent, the people would have starved to death. The article is still in the house on the left as you go in; it is tattered and torn now, as Father or one of the three of us would proudly show it to anyone who turned up.

My mother was an amazing person for growing things. When I was wee, there were always flowers in the house. Down by the beach, yellow irises grew waist-high in huge numbers, the rocks were smothered in sea pinks, and the field behind the house was a multitude of bog cotton, purple from the heather, and primroses on the bank.

She had Father build a small walled garden, where she grew very tall cabbages given to her from a lady who lived in the Fair Isle, and carrots that thrived in the sandy soil.

She knew every bird and creature, and we always had an injured beastie in the house.

Father found an abandoned otter pup one day on Goat Island. He brought it back, and mother fed it on sheep's milk until it was strong enough to manage for itself. It was never part of the family and slept outside, but for all of my youth it would turn up and allow us to scratch it behind the ear and feed it an apple. It was accidentally shut in the house one day, and I'd never seen such a mess. Mother's precious plates were smashed on the floor, and the tartan shawl on the back of the sofa had a big hole in it, where the otter had gripped it in her teeth and thrashed it about.

Mother was also a goddess with the lambing. Late March every year, she would be away for a month across at Borrodale Farm. She would pack her bag, kiss Father and set off with the *cromach* he had made for her twenty-fifth birthday, an ash stick with a Blackface sheep's horn that had been cut, chiselled and sanded into a perfect arc, for her to hold and also to loop around the neck of the sheep to pull it towards her. It had her name – Morag – burned into it.

She had an unusual yellow collie called Flash that she had trained herself and was a great dog altogether, always at her side. Flash really came into her own at lambing time. Mother's small hands were ideal for helping with a difficult lambing; she could slide a hand in and pull the head around inside the ewe, so that it came out first. She had a calming way with her that would settle the sheep down, so they delivered well. The factor knew that if she was there the number of surviving lambs would be high. She was the sort of woman who would be out when the rain had been hammering down for days on end, when just one more walk through the lambing fields to see if everything was all right would be one too many for everyone else. Many is the time that a distressed ewe would be found as a result of her vigilance.

The money that Mother got for the month's work made a real difference to my parents. The job was well paid, and although she was exhausted by the twenty-hour days, she loved it and would come back to the village with a real spring in her step. She always said that she knew winter was finished the day she had her first lamb in her arms. And sure enough, as she walked back to Ardnish from Borrodale she always had primroses in her hands that she had picked on the way.

She got to know all the shepherds in the area, and once a year would head off for the sheepdog trials with Flash and relish the *craic* with the others. I would go with her, but Father never did. 'It's your mother's thing,' he would say.

All the shepherds but one were Catholic, and one, a mild and gentle soul, was called Donnie Macleod and he hailed from Harris. Many of the people from the Outer Isles are known as 'Wee Frees', that is to say that they are members of a Protestant group who don't drink and on the Sabbath nothing apart from praying happens.

The trials were always held on a Saturday, and the shepherds, apart from Donnie Macleod, would go along the previous night, have a few too many drams and talk about sheep. The problem was that the incomer had great dogs, and every year for ten years he would win. The laird of wherever the trials were that year would pass across the ten pound prize money and the cup, and the other shepherds would curse under their breath.

The Friday night get-together was particularly inspired one year. The shepherds decided that Saturday wouldn't do at all, they were all far too busy what with one thing and another, and it would be far better if the trials were moved to the Sunday from then on. Mother and Flash won the next year.

My father Donald John is always called Donald John – never Donald or Donnie. It may seem slightly odd, as Gillies is a MacDonald name, so it is really Donald, son of Donald. There's a man in Kinlocheil called Alexander Alexander, known as Double Sandy. You could never be too serious with my father around; he has a way with him that brings people to a quick smile. He is a kind and generous man, and my mother always said he would take the food from his famished children's table and give it to a stranger rather than let him go on with an empty stomach. She would say, 'It's lucky we don't live on the Mallaig road, with all its passing traffic. We'd have starved by now.'

Father is tall and thin, has a mop of red hair streaked with grey, and a craggy smiling face. He's sixty. He's a piper, and although his fingers are a wee bit stiff now, he used to be the best in the land. He was Pipe Major of the Lovat Scouts before I was born, and hoped that I, too, would be the same. There is no doubt with this background that he was much respected in the area. Everyone knew him, the lairds acknowledged him as one at their level, and when a tune was needed to be dedicated to Queen Victoria on the occasion of her visit to Fort William, it was my father who did the honours.

It is said in the family that I hadn't even reached my first birthday when he had me on his knee blowing into a wee metal pipe that he had made into a chanter of sorts.

'Have you played yet?' he would ask me every morning, almost before my feet had touched the floor beside the bed. Or, as he wrote a new tune, 'Do you think the birrell would do better before the D or after it?'

He soldiered for about half his life, and it was during these years that there was some money around, but these didn't coincide with my life as the regiment was disbanded after the Boer War and resurrected for this war. The beautiful hills and sandy beach around the village didn't make for a living, and when the market for kelp died with the invention of a cheaper chemical that did the same job, half the income of the place was gone. That is when people had to leave.

But not Father. 'I would rather stay here and die than follow Aunt Lexie to Canada, or head off to the shipyards in Glasgow,' he would declare loudly. 'And in any case – "plays the finest Strathspey and Reel in the country" – would having that on my papers secure me a job?' Not to mention the fact that he had a wooden leg, so his mobility was impaired. He did carpentry work at Roshven House quite a lot, creating the panelling and shelving in the library. He took three years to do it, often spending a couple of weeks over there at a time.

He also did some seasonal ghillie work for Arisaig Estate. He had to watch the deer on the hills, establish where they had wandered off to when the stalking was on, and work with the ponies taking the stags back to the larder at the end of the day. The ponies came to him to be saddled up, and he would ride one with his leg sticking out.

The stalker for Ardnish was big Ewen Cameron who lived at Polnish, and it was him my father worked for. Father was paid by the day and didn't work for much more than a third of the year. But we did have the house rent free, and the factor allowed us three cows. Ewen was known as Ewen Fiadhaich, which means wild Ewen, as in his youth he was as wild as a swarm of bees, getting banned from school, often wildly drunk and having tremendous fights over girls.

My mother in her determined way once pleaded with the factor for ways of getting more work to the village. 'Soon everyone will have gone,' she said, 'and Donald John will have us fade away.'

When my father was out with the laird stalking, my mother followed them up and, with big Ewen off gralloching a beast, she told the laird how it was: 'There is a sixty-acre field behind the village, which is too boggy for anything much more than rough grazing. You could make an improvement which would make it possible for us to continue to live there.'

And so it happened. We had eight men come and stay for a month, and with the four in the village helping as well, a massive trench was dug along the middle of the bog, running down to the sea. A high fence was put around the field to keep the deer out, and grass seed was provided for us.

The next year, we had a small farm, with hay and potatoes. My father wrote a letter to the laird saying if he ever had need of a piper he would be delighted to play and would take nothing for it.

The people of the west made money from collecting shellfish. Scallops and whelks were the standard, but razorfish, clams and mussels were also common. They were stored in hessian bags in a flat water pool and sold by the pound whenever a boat came by, maybe once a fortnight. You seldom looked out to sea without spotting a couple of people bent over with a bucket and stick on the foreshore. We could barter the shellfish, too; the driver on the steam train was always happy to swap a couple of bags of good coal for some scallops or mussels, and cousin Tearlach, when visiting from Canna, would arrive with a gallon of fine whisky and leave with some fine fresh lobsters.

Sandy and I would ride the garrons up to the Singing Sands to swim in the summer, or up to Loch Doir a' Ghearrain to try and catch a trout when we knew big Ewen was away. The garron is a Highland pony that is used to carry deer off the mountain. Not a big beast, it is stocky and sure-footed. We usually had two and a foal around the place.

During the rut, with the stags roaring in the hills, the ponies would be alert, knowing that they were to be off up the hill with Father. In the summer months, they might be two hours away on the north of the peninsula. There would be an agreement to meet Ewen Fiadhaich, and father would set off before daylight. In due course, along would come the stalking party – as likely as not a couple of men who had business connections with Sir Arthur. If the day went well, then father would return with news of a stag on the pony and a guinea tip in his pocket. Quite often, they would be stalking on Arisaig peninsula, and the ponies and my father would stay at Borrodale for a few nights.

He never minded; he would have his chanter in his pocket and would play happily for hours by himself.

The peninsula where we live is clothed in heather, with sharp outcrops of lichen-covered rock sticking out of it. When you walked across the hillside you would stick to the paths or the high ground, as the peaty bogs meant the ground could be very wet, and many a time the men would have to pull a cow out of a hole.

To the east is the Rois-Bheinn ridge, the huge boulder-covered, tooth-shaped An Stac and the hills above Inverailort. To our south and west lies the shore. As I lie here it is the sea that I think of most, changing colour daily; with the coral sand making it appear as green as that of the Indies one day and then the next, a heaving black, with the white foam rearing up on the land.

It is on days like these that the stomach churns in fear for the men still out in the boats trying to bring their catch to the shore. There is a village called Smirisary, about four miles beyond Glenuig to the west, where about thirty people live. You couldn't get a cart to it along the rough ground; the houses are scattered around the glen rather than in a row like our village.

All the men there are involved in the fishing. They have two big boats, and they use ropes and wooden tree trunks as rollers to pull them up the steep shingle at the end of the day. The tides dictate the day's activity, as they need to launch and pull the boat in at high tide. It takes four men to work each boat.

One day in late March, the boats went out as usual. But there had been much prior discussion between the men, because although it was calm now, a couple had felt that the weather would turn. My sister Sheena's man, Colin Angus, was among them. Anyway, with money being short they decided to go out. They set off towards Eigg and got the net out to start fishing.

Only half a mile from shore, a squall came in as fast as you can imagine, and everyone on board saw it coming. There was a rush to pull the heavy net in and to turn the bow of the boat towards the wind.

They didn't make it. The heavy net held the boat sideways on, and the waves went straight over the side and tipped the boat. With heavy woollen clothes and the coldness of the water, they didn't have a chance; even if any of them had been able to swim they couldn't have got back to shore. An awful thing, too, was that the people of Smirisary witnessed the whole thing, and couldn't do anything about it.

This was the great disaster of our youth, for Sheena lost the person who was everything to her, and even now, ten years later, she hasn't found herself a husband. Two of the other men were married: one with a wee girl and a wife due shortly, and the second a man near sixty. Also lost was a sixteen-year-old lad, whose mother watched the boat capsize and her son drown. She said that his screams would haunt her until her last breath.

The priest at Glenuig launched a fund to help the dependants, and the *Oban Times* launched an appeal. A lot of the people left Smirisary that year and went to the south. They could not forget that horrible day and needed to start a fresh life.

The people of the west are born with a story always at their lips. My father often told us anecdotes as we gathered driftwood: about the day the seaweed as high as a man was washed onto the beach; or having seen a ghostly deer by the village, evening after evening after a hind was shot by stalkers from the laird's house. Its calf was found by my father and bottle fed. We never tired of the lengthy tale, which could take an hour as he talked in detail of milking the cow for the deer calf and keeping it company in the byre for the first couple of cold October nights. As the calf grew stronger, it followed Sheena and Angus to school and waited outside until they were ready to go home.

Father spoke of our ancestors, and of the great westerly storm of 1760 which blew down all the big trees from Ardnamurchan to Mallaig, and the destruction and misery it caused.

It had come at night when people were in their houses. The roofs were made of heather, of course, and blew straight off. Trees fell on buildings, and even walls that had stood for centuries blew over. Hundreds were killed, and in those days there wasn't a doctor in the area.

Storytelling like this meant that we all knew our history: the bond of our family and its roots. I can see myself in my mind, with a wee lad at my knee beside the fire at Ardnish, telling the same story with the same inflection and exaggerations that my father had.

WAR

I hear Louise talking as she moves around the tent.

'Maybe it'll be quieter tonight,' she whispers to me, and my heart leaps. 'We can talk then.'

The Brigadier doctor is coming to visit from the hospital ship tomorrow, and everyone is working to get the place looking its best. Louise gives me back my shirt, now dry, and helps me to put it on. As she does this I feel her fingers slide up my arm. Or am I imagining it? I might be. I wish I could look in her eyes; then I would be able to tell.

I had a sensation of light in my right eye today. The lids were being held open while being washed, and it was as if there was a flash. It may be a dream, but my head throbs and I have decided that this is a good sign. I may be clutching at straws, but I look forward to when my bandage is next removed. I can't stop myself thinking of things that could happen if my sight was to return. After two weeks convinced that I was dying and that I would be blind to the end, my thoughts now are of proposing to Louise, taking her to Ardnish and becoming a fisherman. I am rushing ahead of reality so I try to caution myself. Just seeing her would be a dream come true. For the first time in days, I fall asleep with a smile on my face.

I wake sometime later, and I am given a cup of tea by one of the male orderlies.

'You look like a happy man,' he said. 'Just what part of this hell hole are you enjoying? The flies, the food, the all-round misery?'

I don't answer but I keep smiling. Unlike his, I thought, perhaps my life is looking better.

Chapter 4

WAR

I keep urging Louise to tell me a bit about herself. Apart from the bare facts I know – that she is Welsh, and a nurse – I hardly know a thing.

Tonight, as the rain thuds against the canvas and there is little other noise apart from the thud and crump of the shells falling in the distance, she tries to make me a bit more comfortable for the night ahead.

'Louise,' I plead, 'tell me about your mother. What's your life like back at home?'

I wait for the inevitable 'Just you go to sleep, boyo, there'll be time for that another day.' Instead, there is silence as she settles herself down beside me. I can smell her, and feel her warmth. She starts to talk in her quiet, considered way . . .

LOUISE

Dad and I had always been close. When I fell and hurt myself, or was unhappy, it was to him I always went. When

I was a baby I was very sick, and he used to hold me throughout the night, willing me to live. I loved him dearly.

We lived in real poverty, although we didn't know it. Sharing an outside toilet with the neighbours, and the five of us children in two large beds. Mam and Dad shared a room with us – how they had the opportunity to have the children God knows.

My parents had always been close. They had married straight out of school and had drawn comfort from each other through the roughest of times. Dad has become quite fat now, his hair is white and greased back, his skin is pale, and the pores are ingrained with the dirt from the mines. He looks like a man twice his age.

We would listen as he coughed. A short sharp hack as he tried to clear the mucus from the back of his throat, then another, and another. His whole body would get caught in the wracking spasm, tightening as he fought for breath. And then, with a great effort, his lungs would release a fistful of phlegm, the colour of the coal that had caused it.

None of us spoke then. Though we were all awake, we lay in fear; a muffled sob from the little one the only sign of the pain we shared with Dad. He'd had the cough, as had most of the men in the town, as long as I could remember. It was only this particular winter that it had got to this stage, and we feared for his life. Mam had been at him to go to the doctor about it, but he wouldn't.

'It's just a winter's cough,' he would say. 'It'll clear up.'

And so we all suffered with him, every morning as he woke for work. Maybe he knew they would stop him going to the pit, and how would he feed us then? There weren't any jobs for a forty-year-old ex-miner.

It was the war that saved us, because at last there was work around. Mam went out to get a job.

'The wee one is eight now,' Mam said, meaning my brother Owen, 'the others can look after him.'

Mam had heard of a cleaning job at the hospital in Abergavenny where her auntie worked. She left the house at five in the morning, walked down to the end of the valley, and took the bus to the town.

After one bad night with Dad not breathing for what seemed like ages, Mam sent me out to get the doctor. Dad didn't know he was coming until he walked in the door, and it was only because of this that Dad agreed to see him.

Thomas, my other younger brother, was sixteen and he got Dad's job in the pit. Mam had fixed it; she went to see the management and told them that Dad wasn't fit for work but the lad would do it. She hated sending Thomas into the mine.

'It's killing your dad,' she said, 'but we need the money. And it's only for a year or two.' That line had been trotted out through the Valleys since the first pit had been sunk. Of course there was no other work, and the money wasn't bad. People preferred not to make the connection between a painful early death and the work.

Life at home became unbearable for the rest of us that summer. Dad got bored and drank too much. He went to the Miners' Welfare Club after he got up and didn't come home till Mam had tea ready at six. Mam tried to control how much money he got, but there always seemed enough for him to get drunk.

Mam excused him. 'It's the pain he's in,' she said. 'He needs to get away from it.'

He wasn't a bad man, he was just in terrible pain.

I remember the night he gave me the puppy. I think he wanted me to know he loved me. Dad knew he had been out of order, and one evening he said, 'Louise, go next door. I've got a present for you. The Bevans are expecting you.'

Owen and I returned with an adorable writhing ball of fluff. It squirmed and licked and ate everything it could get its teeth onto. A wee collie dog, I named him Daffie. Daffie and I went everywhere, even sleeping in the bed between Owen and me.

I was the oldest, and Owen was my charge. I got him up and ready for school after Mam had gone off to work, while Dad lay in bed smelling of the drink and waking only to cough fit to die.

He didn't stir in the morning until we were all out. At night when he was drunk he would shout and smash things in the house. The slightest thing would set him off – tea not ready, the fire not lit – so we would make ourselves scarce. He never hit us but he got more and more irritable, and you could cut the atmosphere with a knife. I could never do anything right and was often crying when Mam came home. My special relationship with my father had gone, and it was me he constantly shouted at to do his fetching and carrying. I wanted to leave, but Mam said she needed me to look after Owen.

*

I pause, swallowing back tears.

'Hard times,' says DP quietly.

He reaches out to me. I think he might put his arms around me, and although there is nothing I want more, I move away a little. The risks are too great.

'Och, DP. I'm talking as if this sort of thing was special to my family, but it's the norm where we live.' I try to keep my voice light, and I can feel my face flushing, but I'm determined to continue with my story ...

*

It wasn't anything specific that put me over the edge, but Dad had been giving me a torrent of abuse since he'd got back from the welfare club, and one day I decided I'd had enough. By the time Mam had come in, the children were all in tears. Dad had stormed out after I'd told him I was leaving. I lay huddled on my bed with Mam beside me as we talked about what I was to do.

In the hospital, there was a notice offering jobs for nurses with the forces. Mam said the Queen Alexandra would get me out of here. 'There must be a better life out there,' she said. She wanted us all to leave the Valleys. Daffie and I went to stay with my aunt in the other terrace, and Dad was told that I'd gone. Thankfully, nobody in the family let him know I was nearby. He sobered up for a few days, and Owen and the others tried to persuade me to come back. I wouldn't. Mam took a day off work, and the two of us went to Newport for the interview. I never went back.

I'd had Daffie for six months by then, and it was him that nearly stopped me signing up. But at least Owen would have him; he adored him.

Three other girls from the Valleys and I went to train at the King Edward VII Hospital for Officers in 9 Grosvenor Gardens, London. The matron was a small tough woman who scared us half to death. She was always immaculately dressed, with not a hair out of place; even her shoes remained impossibly shiny at the end of a day on the wards. Everyone else in the hospital was terrified of her, too, even the surgeon, Colonel Birbeck. Known behind his back as Tommy, Birbeck was the Commanding Officer. If a speck of dirt was found, or we didn't show enough respect to a patient, then all hell would break loose. Matron was posh, too. Her full name was Matron, Lady Viola Dryburgh. She was much older than us, about forty, we guessed. It was rumoured that her brother was an earl. Until just recently, the few Queen Alexandra nurses were all upper-class, but the war had resulted in a massive recruitment, and the likes of me were now allowed to join.

The Queen Alexandra's Imperial Military Nursing Service, to give it its full name, had been a select group of nurses who had to be at least twenty-five years old, but it had been agreed that the numbers be raised to several thousand to cope with the huge demand on the medical services. The matrons were still all upper-class, however.

Sally, one of the trainee nurses, was caught bringing a soldier back to the nurses' quarters. You have never heard anything like it – the soldier in his underwear being chased down the corridor by Matron, with her shrieking like a lunatic. She caught him as he tried to escape through the pantry window. Twice her size, he was shaking like a leaf, as she berated him for twenty minutes until the Military Police came. Sally was given extra duties for months and confined to the hospital. We giggled about it for ages, and no one ever tried to smuggle a man into the quarters again.

Colonel Tommy had a real twinkle in his eye, and when Matron wasn't around he was always telling us stories and teasing us. Now and again, the laughter was heard by Matron, and as she stormed in he would half rise from his seat in apology like a boy caught doing something wrong.

'Staff Nurse Rees, bed pan duty in the Cardigan ward,' she would bark. And then, giving an admonishing glance to the colonel, she would march off.

We were the lowest of the low in the hospital; in fact, the caterers and cleaners had a much better life.

Friday was my day off, but only if we weren't too busy. My friends Madge and Prissie and I would dress up to the nines and head off into Piccadilly and the bars to try and find some officers to take us to dinner or a show.

Madge was beautiful, with long red hair and an elegant figure. She was a surefire way of getting men to join us when we went out, and was seeing a captain in the Hussars who had been a patient. Prissie and I were sure that they were going to get married, although Madge always played it cool with him.

Prissie was petite and very lively, a wonderful character, with sparkly eyes; always playing tricks on everyone. Her hair was jet black and she had naturally dark skin. She hated to go to bed before dawn, and we often ended up dragging her away from dance halls only a couple of hours before we were on duty again.

We had a great time together. There was the fat Frenchman who was far too fresh and who we pushed into the fountain in Trafalgar Square, or the time we ran away from the Military Police and hid behind some bins while all the soldiers were herded into trucks at one particularly rowdy club.

Christmas Eve, and we had nearly finished our training. The three of us were at a bar with a tremendous crowd all around. The band were playing all the favourites, we had danced ourselves half to death, and each of us had a beau. I didn't think life could get much better.

Madge rushed across in great excitement. 'You'll never guess what,' she gasped. 'Matron and Colonel Tommy are here having dinner – just the two of them!'

We moved through the crowd for a closer look, and as we did they got up to dance, passing quite close to us. Matron went right by and didn't see us. Colonel Tommy caught my eye, and I winked at him. He winked back. They danced closely, with me almost cannoning into them once. Matron must have seen us, but she never once looked our way.

The next day we worked awkwardly in her company and nothing was said. The news spread like wildfire, though, and by that night everyone in the hospital knew of their affair.

If only Mam and the rest knew what fun could be had. Mam knew no life outside the Valleys, and that often made me sad.

But the Valleys weren't in my mind that much. We worked from dawn to dusk, night shift every second week; and during our time off we either slept or were with friends. I got letters from Mam the whole time, telling me how the village had been excused conscription because coal was needed for the war, that Dad was poorly, but he got her to read my letters to her over and over again.

I'd been at her to come up to London for a few days and had saved the money for her train ticket, but she said Dad wasn't well enough and someone had to be there for Owen and the others. I was due to finish my training in February, and I got her to promise to come up then. We were to have a presentation of our Queen Alexandra cap badges and a few days off before our postings.

I got a letter from Mam. Dad had collapsed in the welfare club and been rushed to hospital. He had been coughing up blood in the last few days, although he had tried to hide it. She asked if I could get time off to go and see him, saying he'd asked for me. I steeled myself to ask permission. Matron was surprisingly nice about it.

'Of course you can go,' she said. 'Take two days. I'll see if I can get you a warrant for the train.'

I nearly burst into tears, she was so kind.

She only remembered to be tough as I went out the door. 'Don't forget to learn up on limb injuries on the train,' she called out. 'The exam is only three weeks off.'

The exam was all-important. If we passed we would wear the lovely red-and-grey uniform and be respected by everyone; if we failed we would be auxiliaries, doing the menial tasks.

I rushed to get the train to Newport . . .

It took almost seven hours to get there. It would have been a long journey by oneself, but there was plenty of good company.

*

I look closely at DP's face. Not a flicker of acknowledgement that I might be referring to our first encounter. It was so vivid to me, how could he not remember? What I want to say, but can't bring myself to, is this:

The train was packed with a crowd of Highland soldiers off to Brecon for their training. The banter was great, with half a dozen Scouts, as they described themselves, packed into five seats – all full of chat about why the Highlands was the best place to live and how they were off to a posting in the Dardanelles in a month. One of the Jocks was twenty or so, gawky, red-haired and shy; he said it was his first time out of the Highlands. He was a piper; the best there was, the others agreed. As the journey wore on, the others drifted off to sleep or chatted among themselves, and the piper and I had a great blether. He seemed a very kind man. I knew from the start he was special, and I never forgot him.

He told me of the unusual night sky, the northern lights, that he saw at his home. How his dad would wake him before dawn on a cold crisp winter's night and lead him outside, where they would lie side by side on a bank wrapped in a blanket. He described the most extraordinary light show. The sky was lit up with blues and greens and a multitude of colours that swirled and changed, his first recognition of what real beauty was.

It was you, DP, and now I have found you again.

*

I pause, hoping for a reaction, some recognition, but there is none. I tell him I left the train at Newport and took a bus up to Abergavenny . . . I put special stress on 'Abergavenny', still reading DP's face closely. Obviously, the bandages disguise a lot of expression, but, to my intense disappointment, there is still no sign that he remembers once meeting me.

I can't believe he has no recollection. Can he be concealing it? Maybe he's lost his memory since being captured by the Turks. With a heavy sigh, I carry on with my story . . .

*

Mam was in the ward when I got there, dressed in her green cleaner's overalls. I was horrified by how she looked – like a sixty-year-old, with grey unkempt hair, stooped shoulders and a lined face.

Dad was lying on his front, ashen, with a wooden bucket beside him. His eyes lit up when he saw me, and he flopped his arm to welcome me, but he didn't say anything. I leaned over to give him a kiss. He smelled curious – a sweet unpleasant smell – not like Dad. Anyway, that set him off coughing.

I'd forgotten how bad it was. The fit went on for longer than you could hold your breath for, and it was obviously painful as his whole body coiled and uncoiled in physical exertion.

'It will kill him this time,' Mam said and rushed off to get a nurse.

I tried to hold him to me, but he broke free, and it was a good ten minutes before he lay back, dripping in sweat, without an ounce of strength left.

'He's worse,' Mam said, tear-streaked and distraught. 'It won't be long now. Thank God you could make it.'

We both knelt down to pray in the corridor outside his ward. Mam has always been religious. Then we heard Dad starting up again and we returned to his side. My aunt had brought Owen along that afternoon, but Thomas couldn't get off work.

Dad died that night. Mam had left the two us alone while she went to lie down; she'd been sitting up with him for two solid days and nights. I talked to him for ages. I felt I made peace with him. He died in the middle of a coughing fit, his face a look of agony that stayed with him even after the last breath had left his body. I pulled the sheet over his face and wept.

Mam and I got the first bus home in the darkness of the morning.

'It was a year of hell he gave me at the end,' she said, 'but we had twenty great years before that, and it will be those that I will remember.'

The odd thing about a long and painful illness is that death is a relief. My mother seemed to have a weight lifted from her, and the talk was about what she would do now rather than what they had done.

It was great to see the others. Owen was short and solid, always smiling and happy. Mam said Dad was just like that when he was young. Thomas was settled in the mining job and had made some good friends. Mam was so pleased he had been excused conscription, being a miner and all. Don't forget to get a different job after the war, Thomas, she would say every time she saw him. Daffie jumped up and down all over me, but he was Owen's now, I could tell. I loved to see that little dog, though, and it was good for him and Owen to have each other. A weight was lifted from my shoulders, just as it had been from my mother's.

We talked about the future that night. The mining company would want the house empty within a month, now Dad had gone. We would move to Abergavenny, which would get us out of the Valleys and nearer to Mam's work at the hospital. The school was better there, too. Owen wouldn't have to go down the pit – maybe he could even get to university.

'Don't ever come back, Louise, you promise?' Mam said. 'Marry a farmer or a rich man and live an easier life.'

Mam always felt that a farmer's wife was the best thing: plenty of food, land for the wee ones to run around on, and everyone healthy. Miners died so young and painfully; their wives then lost the house and they never had enough money to live on.

Mam asked if I'd met a boy. Was there anyone that had caught my eye? I told her that on nights out with the girls in London there were always men making passes at me, but none was right for me.

'There was an awfully nice soldier on the train on the way here though,' I confessed. 'He's called Donald and he's from the Highlands of Scotland. He's tall with soft red hair and freckles and smiles the whole time. We talked for hours. He told me about the northern lights. He said that, now and again, when the sky is clear and it's a cold winter's night, you can see bright greenish-blue clouds, and the sky lights up. He said his father used to wake him and his brothers and sisters up and take them outside to lie on the beach and look at them. So romantic. He said he wanted to show them to me.'

At least Mam and Thomas had jobs. Mam and I talked about my life in London; she couldn't hear enough about it. She would still come to London when I got qualified, she said. She needed to get away.

I left before the funeral. I had my exam to pass and I was worried about how strict Matron would be about my extended absence. I slept all the way back to London. The exams came and went, and the only one of us to fail was Madge. Too much time thinking about her soldier and not enough work, we thought. Madge would be all right, though, she always was.

*

I want to tell DP that I chose Gallipoli as my posting, because that's where the Scouts had gone. I want to tell him how much I had wanted to meet him again, though meeting him as a patient and one so close to death had not been my plan. With over 100,000 troops down here and a significant number passing through the medical service, it was a miracle we had met at all.

*

Prissie went for the Dardanelles, too, so we would be together. The Queen Alexandra's was recruiting very heavily; they had two hospital ships to find nurses for, no doubt we would be on one of them.

Mam came down for the presentation ceremony. It was the first time she had been out of Wales. We were all as smart as pins in our new uniforms. As we walked along the streets to the Royal Hospital where the ceremony was to happen we enjoyed the admiring glances. Colonel Tommy presented those of us from the King Edward with our cap badges and gave a speech. Two hundred very proud girls that day.

That night we went dancing with our families and friends. It was a wonderful evening. Mam said she felt ten years younger. She had her hair combed back in a bun, and was wearing a pretty dress borrowed from a friend at the hospital. One of the men at the dance had three turns with her that night and we teased her for it. She loved it.

The war had been going on for almost a year by then. Because of the distance back to England, hospitals were set up miles behind our lines, and it was here that almost all the patients who were treatable were looked after. On the Western Front, it was field hospitals – normally commandeered big houses – but in Gallipoli it was hospital ships. The work involved at the Front was harrowing; patients were coming in with limbs blown off, gangrene, gas poisoning. Or dysentery, which was becoming a major problem.

The newspapers were writing full-page stories about the Gallipoli campaign. There had been a lot about the poor medical back-up, how few doctors there were, and how our men at the Front were suffering as a result. It emerged that small boats – lighters – ferried the badly injured men to the ships, going from ship to ship, and a shout would come down, 'All full here'. It broke my heart to hear it. We were desperate to get out there to do our bit.

We were all very nervous, and when my papers arrived a couple of days later confirming not only my destination of the Dardanelles but also the day of sailing in two days' time I felt sick with fear. I can remember it clearly, lying in bed reading page after page of what to take, where to collect my kit, and who to report to and where. Despite stories of the terrible casualties, the disease and lack of water, how the Turks were stopping our men from advancing much beyond the beach, I never regretted signing up.

Matron, who had become like an over-protective mother to us, gave us a talk on the eve of our departure about the temptations of men and the dangers of falling for one of our patients. We laughed it off.

Prissie and I climbed on board a Gibraltar-bound store ship, crewed by a coarse lot from the East End of London. A mutual dislike soon built up. They had a vocabulary so base that my mother's Wesleyan ears would have been burning had she heard them. In return, they thought us prim and stuck up. With us were another seventy passengers, almost all nurses heading down to the war, and a civilian doctor seconded to the army, a Dr Sheridan from London.

We suspected that Dr Sheridan was not a qualified doctor, and wasn't going to the war to help the injured. He couldn't look you in the eye, had a shifty demeanour, and showed no respect for or interest in the soldiers we were going out to treat. He brought with him an enormous quantity of medicine, which he intended to sell to the suffering in Gallipoli: recipes of his own devising, to treat fevers, pneumonia and many other ailments. He showed us his letters of recommendation from all sorts of eminent Harley Street doctors, but neither Prissie nor I believed him.

The very first evening, at tea, a conversation about basic medical practice came up, and that is when I really began to suspect him. Dysentery was the biggest problem in Gallipoli, and we had undergone a considerable amount of training so that we could treat it. Dr Sheridan dismissed it as malingering by men who wanted to get off the front line, and said that in any case, he had just the powder to treat it. We quizzed him about it, but he wouldn't discuss the ingredients, kept saying it was confidential, his own personal mix. What sort of doctor would try to make money out of other people's misfortune? I was horrified by what he was saying and became determined to keep an eye on him, hoping he would perhaps reveal himself to the other passengers as an imposter.

Prissie thought I was exaggerating but agreed we should find out. We planned to set a trap, and sat up late working out a scheme.

One of the other passengers, a Mr Bustin, was an engineer who was going out to advise the army on tunnelling under enemy trenches. He was a very friendly and kind man, and he took a shine to Prissie. We decided to tell him of our suspicions about Dr Sheridan.

We were due to pick up further provisions the next morning in Le Havre. That evening, Mr Bustin wrote a letter to two of the Harley Street doctors who had allegedly provided endorsements to Dr Sheridan, asking them to confirm them or otherwise to the British Medical Authorities in the Dardanelles. We docked in Le Havre at dawn, and Mr Bustin put the letters in the first post.

Over the next two weeks, we constantly challenged Dr Sheridan, to such a stage that he must have suspected something. In fact, he reacted very aggressively to Mr Bustin one night for suggesting that Prissie and I might know more about pneumonia than the doctor himself. By the end of the trip, Prissie was in no doubt of the danger that this impostor posed to the injured soldiers. For instance, what would happen if a severely dehydrated man were to be given one of his pills? He could be so weakened that the slightest negative effects could kill him. It was this background that had made us so suspicious, and when we were in the clearing centre on the beach I hated knowing that he was meant to be treating gravely ill men.

The first port of call was Malta, where half the nurses disembarked. We spent the day there. What a place! Beautiful buildings along the port, where ships ranging from battleships to hospital ships were awaiting refuelling. This gave us our first real taste of what was to come. Prissie and I stood on the quayside as dozens of heavily bandaged men were bought on shore, many with crutches. Stretcher after stretcher went past. We stood in silence, in shock. The men caught our eye and stared blankly at us, their arms often dangling off the side of their stretchers. Many had blood still caked in their filthy hair. Even the nurses looked terrible – gaunt and exhausted – although at least they were going on shore for a few days to recover. As we turned towards each other we realised that we were both in tears. We leaned, sobbing, against a wall, trying to process the horror of what we had seen as it dawned on us that this was only the start. The reality of what our next few months were going to be like was now clear.

Back on board, this time with the deck full to overflowing with ammunition, we headed off to Lemnos, a Greek island about six hours' sailing from Gallipoli. There must have been a hundred boats of various sorts in the bay, where our Gallipoli HQ was located. Apparently, German warships had been sinking many of ours up the front, though, luckily, the hospital ships had been spared so far.

We steamed into Suvla Bay on a hot summer's evening. Many people were out on the deck straining to see what was going on. Prissie and I leaned against the railing and peered through a borrowed telescope.

'Look, Prissie, you can see men moving across the hill over there!' I pointed into the distance. We watched as matchstick men ran through the brush then lay down. Pops of gunfire could be heard crackling across the water. Then the men got up and ran back the way they had come. It didn't seem real.

There were rows of tents on the beach, and small lighters going back and forth with supplies. Horses were teth-
ered in rows along the cliffs. We disembarked onto the
hospital ship, the *Gloucester Castle*, which would be our
workplace and home from now on. There were rumours
that the Turks had overrun the British troops to the east
and a full-scale retreat was on. One of the sailors said that
he was glad we didn't have to land as he feared the boat
would be overrun.

It didn't look too bad from where we were, three
hundred yards away. We could see dozens of men swimming naked. Beyond the sandy beach there were fields, and
some white cottages in the hills. There was a bit of gunfire,
but not too much.

The nurses at Lemnos had told us we had just missed a
period of carnage. There had been a series of big pushes
forward in August and tens of thousands of our men had
been killed or injured. The *Gloucester* had been back and
forth twice to Malta since then, crammed full of injured
soldiers.

We were given a quick tour by Matron and put to work
almost immediately. The procedure was that lighters would
come alongside, and if we had capacity to take more
injured we would. These brave men were manhandled up
the side; usually with a bullet injury; some with severe
dysentery. Apparently, there were medical stations on the
beach, with many more injured than we had on the ship.
The stretcher bearers could give an injection of morphine
and wrap a field bandage on the wounds, but not much
more. The casualty clearing stations treated men who could

be returned to the front line, but operations for bullet or shrapnel wounds were usually treated on the ships. After an attack, there simply wasn't room to handle the volume of men on the ships.

During the month of September, we did a run back to Malta, delivering the injured to the hospitals and collecting supplies. We weren't allowed to carry ammunition, being a hospital ship, but we could bring back food and desperately needed water which we transferred to the stores ship at Lemnos as we passed. With over 300 injured men on board, we worked every hour God gave us. Our only respite came when the ship had to be cleaned from top to bottom in Malta, and then we had three more days as the ship steamed back to Gallipoli.

Dr Sheridan was on our ship, but with several doctors around we didn't see too much of him. He knew to avoid Prissie and me. As we lay in our berths at night we talked about him. We wondered why the authorities hadn't arrested him. Surely he must have been exposed as a fraudster by now?

As we shared our room with another six nurses, soon everyone was in on our suspicion. One of the nurses was seeing one of the other doctors and even told him. Dr Sheridan must have known he was a hunted man by now, but there was nothing more we could do but wait for him to make a major slip-up and hope the other doctors could catch him out.

October arrived, bringing with it a definite feeling that winter was coming. There were frosts at night, and the men were relieved that there were fewer flies around.

I loved my job; we nurses really felt we were making a difference. Until just recently all the medical staff had been male, and the doctors said that we seemed to add that extra touch that made the soldiers feel cared for. Whatever it was, we were told there was a much happier atmosphere on the ship these days. We had no time off and were always exhausted, but I was learning new things every day. I had little time to think of the soldier I had met on the train, but occasionally a Highland voice or the sound of skirling pipes being carried over the water from the shore brought him to the forefront of my mind.

There was talk among the senior officers that Earl Kitchener was thinking of a withdrawal from the entire Gallipoli campaign, though our General, Sir Ian Hamilton, wouldn't consider the idea, I was told. He seemed blind to the unfolding disaster and even wandered around telling everyone how well things were going.

It was late October when we first started getting men in with jaundice. They had yellow eyes, and pale skin, with high temperatures. While not huge numbers, it was one more ailment we could have done without. One of the doctors estimated that about half the soldiers were not really fit to fight now.

When they came on board, assuming we weren't having a rush on, the men would get a bath and be put into pyjamas. Their clothes would be sent off to be cleaned and they would be fed much better than they had been in the trenches. Plus, they would have a comfortable bed. You would think the men would be keen to stay, but on the whole they yearned to get back to their battalions. There was one young officer who was with us three times in as many months: once with a shrapnel wound in the back, and twice with dysentery. After the first injury, without telling anyone, he just climbed out of his bed and climbed into a lighter that was dropping men off. And there was us planning to send him to Lemnos to convalesce!

We'd had a few Lovat Scouts on the ship so far, and no doubt we would have more, as they had only arrived at the end of September. We heard of the considerable success the Scouts had been having over the last few weeks; they had been picking off the enemy officers, resulting in disciplinary problems among the Turks, and there seemed to be a swing of the pendulum in favour of our troops at Suvla.

However, Brigadier General Lord Lovat had himself been stricken down with dysentery and been evacuated to Malta, which was a real blow as people said he was very popular among the men. The other Generals didn't have the oomph that Lovat had. They dithered about an attack while the Turks rushed in reinforcements, meaning we couldn't seize the hilltops. He didn't come on our ship, which was a shame. I would have liked to have met him.

Then we heard that General Hamilton had been sacked by Kitchener. The other officers seemed pleased. He didn't reconnoitre the ground; rather he tried to assess his strategy from maps and from his HQ aboard ship. Perhaps if he had seen the problems the men faced, he would have had different tactics. The word on the officers' wards was of nothing else.

I felt sure we could do more. I spent hours talking to the other nurses and finally came up with a plan. Nervously, I went to speak to the matron about it.

Matron Davy was very professional and looked after us well. She and I got on just fine. She listened as I explained my ideas. Perhaps some of the nurses could go onshore and join the medics who were really struggling to cope at the Casualty Clearing Station on the beach? The need was so desperate, surely we could do more good there?

But she wouldn't hear of it. She said we would be in danger and there wouldn't be accommodation for us. She told me to leave it at that, but said we would talk about it again in a few days. I was determined now, however, and as my Mam would tell you, when I want to do something I usually end up doing it.

Anyway, the nurse who had the doctor friend told him what I'd requested and he in turn told the Brigadier doctor who commanded the ship's hospital. As a result, Matron and I were marched in to see the Brigadier.

'Well, Staff Nurse Jones, I gather you have a plan. Would you like to tell me about it?' he said, not unkindly.

'Well, sir,' I stuttered, 'the problem seems to me that the Casualty Clearing Stations are not set up to deliver the medical service they could. And if soldiers were treated better and quicker there, we would have a far higher survival rate, and the backlog of men waiting to get to the hospital ships would be a lot less.'

Matron Davy responded with all the objections she had put to me two days before, though not so forcibly with the Brigadier. The one point he seemed unable to respond to was who could authorise the Queen Alexandra nurses to do a shore-based job, with the danger of coming under fire. Yet there was no doubt that he was persuaded, and I was told to go and continue with my duties while he and Matron spoke. Later in the day I saw the matron and asked her how things had turned out.

'If there is any decision, you will hear about it in due course, Staff Nurse Jones,' she said stiffly, and walked on. We all respected Matron – she worked tirelessly and was very good at her job – however, she didn't mix well with us new nurses and definitely saw us as lower-class.

There was talk of nothing else among the nurses. On balance, they were keen to go and help on shore, wondering whether perhaps a rota could be set up, such as two days on shore and then two days on the ship, for a trial period. Communication between the Queen Alexandra nurses' HQ on Malta and the front line always took a while.

A whole week passed, during which we heard nothing. But things finally came to a head when the ambulance boats reported that many of the medics at the Casualty Clearing Station had come down with dysentery, and there were not enough people to manage.

I spoke to Prissie, and together we decided to corner the Brigadier. We waited outside the officers' mess until eventually he beckoned us into his office.

'How about we just climb into the lighters now, sir? No one would stop us. The men at casualty will be in a terrible way. They *need* us.'

He paused, then smiled and nodded. 'We never had this conversation.'

With our hearts beating fit to burst, we rushed back to our berths. At dawn, we agreed, we would get the first boat going ashore. We asked Mary and Lorraine to join us; they had been keen when we had originally floated the idea.

Thus it was that at five in the morning, we four were in our tidy scarlet uniforms, with a box of medical equipment, stepping confidently onto the lighter.

'Doing a task for the Brigadier doctor,' I said primly, as we sat down.

The sergeant just nodded.

Fifteen minutes later, we parted the curtain of the largest tent and were confronted by the sight of dozens of men lying on camp beds and the ground. There was a look of surprise from everyone, and then a cheer went up so loud that others came to see what was going on.

Our faces were pink with embarrassment, but our chests swelled with pride at the welcome. A doctor came across to us, and we explained that we were there to help.

'By God, we need it,' he said. 'I've had no sleep for two nights, and we're down to three of us, with two hundred injured and more coming in all the time.'

There were twenty canvas bell tents, a kitchen and store tent, and a marquee to treat the newly arrived. Within minutes, we had arranged big vats of boiling water and were unwrapping bandages, putting on antiseptic creams, using scalpels to cut off bits of gangrene and generally doing all the work and more that we had been doing on the *Gloucester*. After two months, we could do most of the practical work that the doctors did, anyway. Yet, although we never would have expected it, I think that just our being there and caring for the men was the most important part of it all.

Sometimes, the sea was too rough for the small boats, and the lighters would be nowhere to be seen. Occasionally, they came back with the injured men when the hospital ships were full and they were turned away. We felt like crying with frustration when we knew they could have saved a man on the *Gloucester*, but here we were only three hundred yards away, unable to get him onboard and watching him die.

What would normally have been the job of the ship's surgeon became ours as we held the fort. Digging a bullet out of a man's leg when he had been injured for three days with his leg swollen to twice its normal size brought forth tears of gratitude. He held my hand and whispered his thanks, even though our work doubled the pain he was in already.

We did days of this, non-stop. The patients were from Norfolk, Ireland. There were Gurkhas, Aussies – all cheerful and grateful. Our uniforms were soaked in blood and covered in dirt, and we were exhausted but we felt elated, too.

During a lull, us four nurses sat outside a tent in the weak autumn sun with a cigarette and a cup of tea and talked.

'My lord, if my George could see me now,' Lorraine exclaimed. 'Filthy hair, mud and blood everywhere, broken nails – he'd go back to his old girlfriend in a jiffy!'

We all laughed. We all looked the same.

One morning, the Brigadier doctor appeared suddenly beside me. 'Jolly well done, Nurse Jones. I gather you are the heroine of Suvla – we should call you Florence

Nightingale. I have another half a dozen nurses on the next boat, so you and your girls can go back to the ship and find your beds. We haven't heard from the Queen Alexandra HQ in Malta yet, as it happens, but you can assume that you have done the right thing. The men are all the better for it.'

Later that morning, the four of us stepped back onto the *Gloucester Castle* and were met by many nurses and doctors all keen to shake our hands. Even Matron Davy looked us in the eye and congratulated us.

'You did the right thing,' she said and smiled. 'It made a huge difference to the men on the beach, and we are proud of you.'

Overjoyed, we ate a huge meal, had a thorough scrub and went to our cabin to sleep for twelve solid hours.

Chapter 5

WAR

Louise is off duty now. It is night, and with dawn not far off, the place is quiet apart from some murmuring in the tent next door. I dangle my hand in the sand below the camp bed and wave at the flies buzzing around my head. It is cold. But at least I have blankets; the men in the trenches will be freezing.

I have been avoiding the issue, not confronting what happened to me. I have always tended to look for good things and avoid unpleasant ones, so my mind wanders to Ardnish or Louise. I blank out my pain. All of the other men in here were either shot or hit by shrapnel from the shelling. In the other tents there are men who have dysentery.

I find it painful to think about Sandy. After my family, he had always been my closest friend, and of course what happened to him took place at the same time as I was injured.

Sandy was a gangly fellow, always smiling, with a friendly word for everyone. That's not to say he didn't have a temper. It's just that it was slow to come, and when it did, you were as well to keep your head down, for as quickly as it appeared it was away again, and he had forgotten all about it. He had black hair and a very fair complexion, which took a lot of punishment from the Mediterranean sun. He didn't talk much and was far more thoughtful than me, though when he did speak he was worth listening to. We were very close. It was the fishing that was his true passion. He would sit with his rod for hours waiting for a bite, whereas I was always itching to be at something else. We were as different as chalk and cheese: he excelled at school while I was always in trouble; he would help with the chores while I was up to mischief – allegedly. He was as good as a brother to me and much closer than Father Angus, who was just that wee bit older.

Orders were given from above that there was to be a big push. We were issued with extra ammunition and told to be on standby for a 6 a.m. assault. As we understood it, in normal battles there would be some massive shelling on the enemy position, a cavalry charge would go through, and then us infantry. But this time there would just be us.

We stood in our trenches as the sun broke through. Officers dashed back and forth with orders, as sergeants handed out ammunition and barked at youngsters to do their laces up and cheer up.

My stomach was churning with fear. 'God smile upon us, look after us,' I prayed. 'Please may the Generals know what they are commanding us to do.'

We were given the order to fix bayonets. I pumped up my bagpipes, and then, on the command 'Charge!', I launched into the tune 'Highland Laddie' and stepped onto the parapet.

The men charged out of our trenches, the Turkish machine guns opened fire and then, horribly quickly, at least half of our men were slaughtered. Not one of us even made it to the barbed wire in front of their trenches. It was the most dreadful episode. After only a matter of minutes, Captain Mackenzie shouted, 'Retreat, retreat!'

There is nothing that can prepare anyone for this: the futility and senseless murder of men yet to experience the best days of their lives. Did the officers giving the orders truly have any idea what they were doing? Did they not know the Turks had machine guns facing down the hill at us, that we had barbed wire we had to clamber through? In the army, we are trained to believe that 'they' – meaning the officers – know best, that they have a plan and that we are a key component part of that plan.

Those of us in Gallipoli will never believe that again.

We came out of what little cover we had and ran back to our lines, with the machine guns mowing us down all the while. Men stooped to grab their injured friends in no man's land, and drag them back to the trench only to be shot themselves. Ewan Anderson from my troop had his arm under his brother Iain's shoulder, half lifting, half dragging him to our lines. Men were shouting, 'Come on, come on!' They were so close. Then some sadistic bastard gave a short burst of machine-gun fire and sliced them down in front of us. Hundreds of injured were left between the lines.

And then the Turks lit the dried grass, and a fire swiftly approached our injured men who were trying to drag themselves towards us. With thick smoke in our eyes, we could barely see over the parapet of the trench. I can still hear the screaming of the men as the fire engulfed them.

During our training we were told again and again that unarmed men helping the injured, not only the stretcher bearers, must be left alone. I can honestly say that not one of our men would have done otherwise before today. The despicable behaviour of the Turks has shocked us all.

That night, our battalion was taken back from the forward trenches to get some rest on the beach for a couple of days. Lord Lovat walked among us, clearly in shock, though we knew the attack had been ordered from above him and he was not to blame. There was little talk between the men. We simply lay in rows, privately reliving the horror of that morning.

A few days later, Sandy and I were chosen, along with Sergeant MacLeod and Tommie Mackay, to conduct an assassination of a top Turkish colonel. It wasn't the leader, Kamal, but another one; we didn't catch his name. We were only told that he would arrive on a horse with several fellow officers accompanying him and he would have red epaulettes and a sword at his belt. Colonel Willie had heard that he was due to visit his troops and that he always walked among his men. So, an opportunity to get him was pretty high.

Sandy was said to be the best shot in the battalion, and it was he who was expected to pull the trigger.

Obviously, a great sniper has to be accurate, but equally as important is his ability to lie completely still, without the flicker of an eyelid almost. The sweat pours off the face in the heat of the day, and the flies stop buzzing around only to bite you, resulting in large red lumps in which they have laid their eggs. The great sniper lies all day, impervious to all this, waiting for that second where the enemy moves first, his position is exposed, and the trigger is squeezed.

We spent a day working out our plan of attack, and a night reconnoitring our route in. The plan was to move under the cover of darkness to a hillside which had a good view over the Turkish headquarters, where over a hundred soldiers were camped. It was a plan fraught with danger, as the ideal firing spot was only twenty yards from their observation post, and with the General around, they would be more vigilant than usual.

We moved through our front line shortly after one in the morning, with messages of good luck from the men in the trenches. The Scouts' success at this sort of thing had been widely recognised, and news that a big hit was on had spread, too, though hopefully not as far as the enemy.

The Turkish HQ at Suvla was about a mile beyond enemy lines, behind a hill called Tekke Tepe, part of an old farm. On the top of the hill was an observation post where the Turkish officers could survey the hills around and look down on the beaches and our positions with their binoculars.

We went out on a big flanking sweep along the seashore, slipping on seaweed and scrambling to get a grip along the crumbling cliff face that ran straight down to the sea in places. Then up the hill into position, well behind the Turkish-held ground.

It took us three hours to reach the spot from where the final approach was to be made. Not a murmur was heard, just the occasional crack of a twig which made us crouch and freeze for a couple of minutes. Although we knew where their sentries were, we knew they would have patrols out, too. At one stage, the sergeant signalled for us to take cover, as he heard the murmur of voices. A dozen Turks approached, heading for our lines.

We hugged the ground, with my heart pounding so hard I thought they must hear it. How they didn't see us, I'll never know. In the moonlight we could see individual features. We only had an hour before dawn, and half a mile of a very tricky approach still to make. With nothing but two rifles and three pistols between us, and a water bottle strapped to our belts, we were able to crawl relatively easily through the undergrowth. Nevertheless, in the stillness of the morning it appeared that we were making a considerable noise.

I prayed that the Turks were drowsy towards the end of their sentry duty. We could see the knoll that we had identified the previous night as the spot for their observation post. With our faces down, we inched up the hill until we were behind the clump of thorn bushes which we intended to hide in.

Getting in wasn't easy. Our hands and faces were covered with scratches from the thorns by the time we made it. There wasn't much room in the small copse. We lay, facing out at different angles, to watch out for the enemy. Sandy moved forward to the edge, to a position from where he could take his shot.

Our position seemed excellent: the thick leafy bushes gave tremendous cover from the view of the observation post, as well as shelter from the heat of the midday sun. The 200-yard distance from the hill above the enemy HQ was ideal for Sandy to get his shot off.

There was only one problem, one of which we were all too aware. Effectively, we were on a suicide mission. With the enemy position right beside us, we were going to be sitting targets for their Gatling gun; we knew that its 200 bullets a minute pouring into our bush would spell the end for us. But Colonel Willie had told us of the necessity of getting the Colonel.

'If he is dead,' he said, 'this could well turn the war in our favour. We have chosen our best men for the job.' And then, to me, as we set off, he said, 'Make sure you come back, my piper. I need you.'

Sergeant McLeod had devised a plan that would at least give us a chance: the second the shot was fired, the rest of us would make a dash for the observation post with our pistols and bayonets, and try to get them before they could see that we were in the bush right in front of them. We would then make our escape down the back of the hill, and Sandy would follow as best he could.

Dawn broke to the sound of movement in the camp below us. Fires were lit and coffee brewed. Four Turks came up to relieve those in our neighbouring position, carrying mugs with them. The smell drifted across to us. And so, with much loud discussion and a sharing of a cigarette, the night watch headed back to camp. At least we now knew their numbers.

We lay there as quiet as mice, the sweat pouring off our bodies, careful not to move. Having had a sleepless night, I became drowsy in the heat. We had been in position well before dawn, so I had been unable to move at all for ten hours. I was worried about getting cramp, and I couldn't even turn my head to look at Sandy, who was peering down the barrel of his gun.

The first we would know of anything up would be the crack of Sandy's rifle, and then we would be up and charging at the observation post. I fought to stay awake and alert. My thoughts drifted back to home. What would Mum be doing now? Was Dad all right with his bad leg? It would be the hind stalking now, he would be limping off with his garron to meet the stalking party. The hay and potatoes would be in for the winter and the peat cut and drying behind the house. They must be struggling without Sandy and me there; before the war we had done a lot of the heavy work. If I shut my eyes and concentrated really carefully, I could envisage myself there.

I let my mind wander further. Mother would be a bit lonely now with all her family gone. She'd also be the youngest person in Peanmeanach. The school had closed, and there was only a handful of old folk left in the village. She would be knitting; she usually is. I got a letter from about her two weeks ago. They seemed well, but you could sense the worry she had for Angus and myself.

There was another change of shift. The Turks' observation post now had eight men in it. They stood and smoked and talked, so close we could hear every word. Half of them set off back to their camp. It must be mid afternoon by now; I was getting hungry. Maybe the Colonel wouldn't come today; perhaps we would still be here tomorrow. The flies were not too bad now. A month ago, they would have been everywhere. In the summer, in our trenches with the dead bodies around us, when you received your food the top of it was a mass of flies within seconds. As Sandy and I lay there, we couldn't do anything to brush them off – a flick of a head or wrist might alert the enemy.

Sandy murmured, 'I can see him clearly. I'm going to shoot.'

Even with his warning, I still jumped about three feet in the air when the shot was fired, and scrambled to get up.

Sandy fired twice more. I broke through the bush, brandishing my pistol as I rushed for the Turks' observation post to our right.

I saw a terrified face and caught sight of a rifle being raised. I saw him struggling to wrench the gun round towards us, a flash of steel and then an enormous thump. I had been shot in the shoulder. I spun round and fell. Their machine gun fired a burst, then I heard shouting and several pistol shots.

I could taste blood, and everything went dark. In my subconscious I could hear my mother talking to me: 'Come into the house now. Everything will be all right. Come and sit on my lap, try and sleep.'

Once, at home, there had been a terrible accident. I had found a body on the beach, up towards Singing Sands. It was Fraser, Sandy's father, lying in the seaweed, the waves pushing him up, then pulling him back with their movement. He was still hanging onto the oar he had been washed up with. He must have fallen overboard and died of exposure. His wife and Sandy were running down the hillside – her terrible keening, the wail piercing the heart like nothing I will hear again.

I was ripped out of my nightmare, only for it to be replaced by a real-life one. My eyes snapped open as I was hit. I could make out the sallow skin of the Turk, his black eyes boring into me. Again, his fist smashed into my stomach.

I lay retching. My right arm hung useless from its badly injured shoulder. Another Turk stopped my assailant and pulled me into a sitting position.

I knew I was going to be beaten up, although what I could tell them that was of any use was unclear. The Turks had developed torture into a fine art, and I was going to be the next victim upon whom they could develop their sadistic expertise. My mind slipped back to home where Johnny had come over to take a look at my tooth. It was one of the back ones and it had gone rotten. The side of my face was hugely swollen, and I was in agony. The Bochan was the expert at this on Ardnish peninsula, and rather than go and see the expensive dentist in Fort William and spend all day getting there and back, everyone gave the Bochan a shout. I was just a wee fellow then and didn't know what to expect. He tied a blindfold over my eyes, Mother held my hand, and then he put a length of fishing line around the tooth. When I least expected it, there was a crash and mighty yank as the door was slammed and the tooth was ripped out and catapulted across the floor.

I was jerked back to real life, and agonising pain. I remember clearly the first half an hour of being thumped and kicked in and out of consciousness, and then their officer went away and the level of brutality increased even further.

There was an open fire and a pot of boiling water. One of the Turks seized it and threw it across my face. I heard myself let out a scream, and then there was silence as I blacked out.

I remembered nothing for a considerable time. I was lying in a foetal position on the ground. My face was throbbing, my eyes were hellish sore, and the searing pain was heightened by the fact that I couldn't see if it was dark or light. My entire body felt pulverised, with my right shoulder in particular in a bad way. We must have been inside a farm building; I could smell the familiar scent of musty hay.

Then, over time, I became aware that I was not the only person lying there. I could hear moaning, and a rattle as breath was inhaled and exhaled through near-defunct lungs. The person tried to speak. It was in Gaelic. At first I didn't know who it was, then it became clear – it was Sandy. I rolled over towards him, onto my injured shoulder, causing such a spasm of pain that I again lost consciousness.

When I came to, Sandy's face was right beside mine. We spoke falteringly about the events of the last few hours, how he had succeeded in getting the Colonel, how maybe it would help in turning the war our way. They knew I was a goner, they had seen me go down. The others had shot the four Turks and then sprinted off back the way we had come. They had become separated, and Sandy had found a bush he could lie up in until darkness. As soon as it was dark, he set off again. He had been so close to getting away. If the flare hadn't gone up at the exact moment that he was rushing head-long down the gulley, back towards our own troops, he would have made it. Or if there hadn't been a Turkish patrol right there at the time. The Turks returned to camp to hear of the death of the Colonel, and then they had tortured him. His testicles had been cut off, and he was bleeding heavily.

We spoke about Ardnish and the best days of our life. He said less and less, his voice growing quieter. I held his hand and knew he was dying. I gave him the last rites, struggling to remember the words my brother had used after Sandy's own father had drowned. Was it only last year?

'*Imich as an t-saoghal seo, O anam Chriosdail, ann an ainm Dhe an t-Athair . . .*'

'Go forth, Christian soul, from this world in the name of God the Father . . .'

Tears ran down my face as his soul slipped gently away to God, then I wept for myself and the pain I was in. And then in my homesickness I sobbed for his mother and the people of our village who held him so dear.

Men came to check up on us and saw that Sandy had died. They went off again. Later, one came back and gave me water. I don't know why as he must have been expecting me to follow Sandy soon. I know I was. He held my head up and tenderly poured water from his bottle into my mouth. Then he made a pillow from a jacket, probably Sandy's, all without a word. It is funny how when the Devil is in everyone and Hell is where we are, there often appears a saint whose ray of godliness brightens our world.

Much later, more shooting started. There was the sound of panic-stricken Turks shouting and people running past the enclosure where I lay. And then I heard my name being called in Gaelic. I responded weakly, but they didn't hear me, so I lay there hoping, praying. The voices moved off; the shooting became more distant. I could hear no one now. They were chasing the Turks, I guessed. The lads will guess we have been tortured, so there won't be much quarter given for them, I thought. Footsteps entered the steading, and then Sergeant McLeod was saying, 'We'll soon have you home, young Gillies. I'll just get the lads to make a stretcher.'

When he returned he asked what had happened to Sandy. I told him. I also told him about my shoulder, the beating I had undergone, and the boiling water thrown on my face. He was horrified. I think if any Turks had been captured then, it would have been difficult to stop the soldiers from shooting them.

Soon the rest of the Scouts returned. None of them had been shot and they were very cheerful with their success in routing the Turks until Macleod told them about Sandy's death and my torture. A stretcher was made by threading poles from the Turkish tents through their coat sleeves, and I was lifted onto it. While this was happening, a grave was being dug for Sandy. They decided they couldn't carry his body back to our own lines.

The trip back was hellish, even though I was drifting in and out of consciousness for most of it. My ribs were sore on the opposite side from my bloody shoulder, so whichever side I lay on, I was in real pain. There is no doubt at that time that death would have been preferable. The Scouts took turns to carry the stretcher, cursing as they stumbled and fell. The trip took an eternity.

I was told later that Colonel Macdonald was nearly court-martialled for sending the rescue party in for Sandy and me, for exposing a whole troop to danger for the sake of two men who were almost certainly dead. It was this sort of thing which made the other soldiers so envious of the Scouts, and I was profoundly grateful for his actions.

Chapter 6

LOUISE'S JOURNAL

Earl Kitchener, the Secretary of State for War, has travelled here, and is based on the battleship *Lord Nelson* anchored beside our own *Gloucester Castle*. I saw him from a distance. He seems very popular with the men. We're experiencing strong winds and heavy rain every few days, and are preparing for winter. Wriggly tin and wooden spars are being unloaded to reinforce the trenches. The horses and mules have blankets now.

Our rota's working well, and the mixture of time at the Casualty Clearing Station and on ship makes everything bearable.

I was onshore, helping with an operation on a man's foot, with the dreaded Dr Sheridan handling the scalpel. As usual, he never looked me in the eye. I itched to take the knife from him. I just can't trust him to use it properly.

The tent flap opened, and a Lovat Scout officer said that a good man was coming in, he was in a bad way, and that I was to look after him. The stretcher bearers were exhausted, sweat pouring down their faces. They seemed to have carried the man a long way. He was laid on the floor of our operating tent and Dr Sheridan felt his pulse.

I looked over his shoulder and it was as if I had been punched. I recognised Donald Peter, my soldier from the train. He was unconscious, with his red hair soaked with sweat, and a ghastly sheen on his face where he had been terribly burned.

I stood in shock, mouth open, as he was laid on the operating table. I felt faint and had to be helped to a chair by one of the soldiers. I told him I'd be fine and composed myself as quickly as I could.

Dr Sheridan was cutting his shirt off. ' I can feel his pulse, but only just,' he said.

DP was barely conscious. 'I'm not sure if we can save this one,' Dr Sheridan said. I couldn't disagree. We'd had many on the operating table who'd looked a lot better and still died. My professional training took over and I was soon busy with boiling water and instruments.

DP's shoulder was terribly swollen, with a hole so big in the scapula you could almost put your hand in it. Bits of bone mixed with blood were flecked on his green shirt. Dr Sheridan decided to operate immediately.

Luckily, a senior doctor arrived and took charge. I felt overwhelmed with relief that DP's life would not lie in the hands of Dr Sheridan.

We feared that the shock of the operation would kill him, but we knew it wouldn't be long before gangrene settled in if we didn't, so there was no real choice. We had to act quickly.

'His heart's too weak for morphine,' the doctor pronounced, to my horror. And so four male medics were called to hold him down while the cutting was done. As the knife started to cut out the damaged flesh, he woke with a loud scream, bucking and twisting with amazing strength. We were terrified that he might throw us off and he would end up on the floor.

I had to turn my head away, so the medical staff wouldn't see the tears pouring down my face. Mercifully, DP lapsed back into unconsciousness and, after quite a struggle with the forceps, a bullet was found and removed. It had twisted and followed a bone down into a muscle alongside his spine.

Later on, I decided not to tell anyone but Prissie of my previous meeting with DP. I knew I would not be allowed to nurse him if Matron knew. But I knew that I cared for this man – just a few hours on a train and yet I remembered every second. Pity, and the yearning to help him, only compounded my wish to take him in my arms and hold him. But I couldn't. I was too scared. This was not how I had imagined our reunion.

The next twenty-four hours were going to be crucial if DP was going to live. Fortunately, there was a lull in new admissions and so I was able to concentrate on him. I sat beside him throughout that first night, to stop him rolling onto his injured side and to bathe his brow with cool water. He was delirious, and kept calling out in Gaelic, words that were unintelligible to me. At times he would lie motionless with his eyes wide open. They were in a dreadful condition, more like red welts filled with pus. Matron had decided that they should remain unbandaged to allow them to dry and heal better, and also allow us to monitor their condition for the first day or two. We used white salve on his burns to lessen the pain.

One time, when my face was only a few inches from his, I felt his hand come up and rest briefly on my neck, but I didn't know if he was aware of what he had done.

Everyone was surprised that he survived the first night, but he was certainly still in danger. His commanding officer, Colonel Macdonald, came by to visit, and spoke to him in Gaelic for a long time before going. I don't think DP heard a word of it, though.

But the fever had definitely gone from him. He'd stopped shaking and would take a little of the porridge I spooned into his mouth.

After many hours, Prissie was told to relieve me, and Matron marched me to the nurses' tent with firm instructions that I was not to reappear until the next morning. My mind was in turmoil and it was ages before I drifted off into an exhausted sleep. Was he going to live? Had he recognised my voice, realised who I was? Had anyone said my name? He couldn't see, obviously, and he wouldn't know I had also been posted to Gallipoli. I decided, with a twinge of sadness, that he was almost certain not to know and, though it broke my heart, I wasn't going to tell him.

I couldn't wait to tell Prissie everything, though. That night as we lay in our camp beds, I told her that DP was my Highland boy from the train, that we had a special connection. Did she remember when I went to my Dad's funeral?

Prissie was astonished. She was so kind. She wished me luck and held my hand tightly, but she did say that falling for a half dead man wasn't a good idea.

DP slowly improved over the next couple of days. His fever subsided, and he regained consciousness. I spent several hours a day at his bedside, talking about everything you can imagine. He spoke little at first, reconciling himself to his injuries, and building up his strength. I fed him mashed food and gave him boiled water, and he often slept twelve fitful hours at a time. His dreams were horrid and violent, and his body would twist to and fro, often damaging the tissue that was repairing during the day.

He would shout out Sandy's name and the names of his family. He would plead for his captors to leave him alone, then he would cry silently. I shared his pain and wept along with him, though I was careful not to let anyone see me.

I thought back to the train journey and wondered if it had just been a passing attraction. We had only spoken for a short time, really, on that train back to Wales. But since then, I had often dreamed about him and wondered what had happened to him in the ensuing months. Now he was in my care, and I was as close to him as you could get. My friends back home in Wales would have been practically measuring me up for my wedding dress, had they known how I felt.

A new Scottish General, Sir Hector Munro, arrived, and there were rumours that a retreat was being considered. Certainly there were no new troops arriving, so DP got more than his fair share of attention. I was sure that he would soon be sent to the hospital ships, but, apart from one, they hadn't yet returned from taking casualties to Malta. I was fairly sure I would be able to get on whatever ship he was on, anyway, I was well enough known by now.

About two weeks had passed since DP had come into the Clearing Station, and he was different from the broken, scarred and silent man I saw after his capture. His face was still a mess, but it was scabbed rather than looking like livid raw meat. His shoulder was healing well, and best of all it seemed that he might get some sight back in his right eye. He wasn't strong by any means but I felt sure he was going to live. We had an easy rapport now, enjoying each other's stories and company.

Thankfully, Dr Sheridan and I were working together less often. He was mainly in the operating tent and I was in the recovery tents. Occasionally though, he would do a round. One morning, I noticed he was holding a tube of some thick yellow paste, which he seemed determined to force down DP's throat.

I asked him what it was, and he said that it was vitamins and minerals, to build his strength. His own concoction, he volunteered. As usual, he wouldn't catch my eye.

I told him in no uncertain terms that I was not happy about it, but he ignored me. I knew I could not let him continue, so I repeated what I'd said and told him I was going to get the senior doctor for a second opinion.

He became flustered and strode out of the tent. He had probably never been challenged like that before.

I was shaking and desperately needed to sit down. On the edge of DP's bed, I covered my face with my hands, I was desperate to reach out for his hand, for his support, but didn't. We had an audience. Many of the other men in the ward had seen my act of defiance and were clearly on my side, but I prayed I wouldn't be reported for insubordination and sent back to the ship. I was counting on the fact that he wouldn't want too much attention on himself and his potions.

But even as I recovered myself, I knew I had become even more determined to expose him.

The 26th of November brought disaster. An enormous storm hit us. Torrential rain and gale force winds hit at tea-time and again two hours later when it was dark. Tents were blown down, causing misery to the injured men inside. All who were able rushed outside and did their best to put in new posts and hammer pegs back in. But the ground became so wet and soft that the pegs were just ripped straight out again. The big tent was completely shredded and lay flapping in the wind. Everyone was soaked and miserable.

The next day, it continued. Relentless freezing rain and sleet with 70mph winds. To make matters worse, the Clearing Station started to get very busy, with a steady stream of men coming down with exposure and exhaustion. We had managed fairly well with 200 patients, but by the night of the 28th we had over 800 men seeking help and shelter. The three cooks did an incredible job providing tea and hot food for everyone. That night, the rain turned to snow and the temperature dropped to −18. Apparently, five soldiers who had tried to take shelter were found dead the next morning, their soaking uniforms frozen solid. No wonder we saw so many casualties.

We desperately needed to get men onto the ships as soon as possible, but the sea was too rough for the ambulance boats to work. The beetles were best for the job, being covered, but they didn't hold many. It was eventually decided that we would send some men back, and myself and DP were to be on one of the first boats.

I told DP that we would be leaving that afternoon.

'What about my pipes?' DP asked. 'Can we take them?'

I had to tell him that there probably wouldn't be any room.

Later, DP called me over and asked if we could write 'Colonel Macdonald, Lovat Scouts' on them. Then, there might be a chance they'd get to him. He'd know whose they were.

I agreed, and told him I'd put them in the headquarters tents. I knew how much they meant to him. The Colonel wasn't exactly well, either, however. He was suffering from dysentery, and important though the pipes were to DP they surely wouldn't matter much to his CO. If there was a retreat from the peninsula, space would be at a premium, and I felt sure the pipes would be left behind. Still, DP seemed pleased and confident they would be in safe hands and that, for now, was what mattered.

Prissie came on the first boat out, too, along with Dr Sheridan, a couple more medics and fifteen injured soldiers. Sailors held the boat steady as we loaded the men, wading out waist-deep into the waves. We were about halfway across the 800 yards to the *Gloucester Castle*, I guessed, with the boat being thrown about like a cork, when there was a huge wave and water began pouring in through the hatch. There was much shouting from the sailors. The struggling engine missed its beat, and after a minute it packed in. Our hearts were in our mouths, with not a word from the anxious passengers.

A couple of the sailors were in the hold with us, with the cover off the engine, cursing about water in the fuel. We couldn't see anything, and felt helpless as the waves crashed relentlessly on top of us. There was about a foot of freezing water in the hold by now, and we were soaked. A man was standing on the deck and waving, trying to catch the attention of other boats so we could get a tow.

An injured officer pulled himself onto the deck to see what was going on. He told us that we were drifting parallel to the shore, that he could see the ships but they were a mile away.

I put my arm around DP and pulled a blanket around his shoulder. He was shivering so badly with the cold.

Then, one of the sailors shouted that we were heading for the rocks and we'd have to get out as quickly as possible. It was terrifying. We just sat, surrounded by the noise of the sea and the commotion from the deck as the sailors tried to manoeuvre the boat using oars. But it was hopeless. With a great crash and the sound of ripping wood we thumped into the rocks. What seemed like an eternity passed as the beetle was dragged by the sailors out of the worst of the surf and we were helped out through the waist-high waves onto the safety of the rocks – though they were treacherously slippy with the water freezing on top of them.

Despite there being a man on each side of DP, he slipped and fell again and again as he blindly inched his way forward. He wore a sling on the injured side, so he couldn't put an arm out to protect himself if he fell. He was in a lot of pain, wet and cold and shaking like a leaf.

We crawled in the evening light to the relative shelter of the cliffs to try to escape the snow. The sailors had rescued a canvas tarpaulin from the beetle and, using the oars, a windbreak was erected. There was no food or means of making a fire. Everyone huddled against each other and a miserable cold night dragged by. This was the first time DP had walked anywhere since he'd arrived at the Clearing Station. I knew that if we were going to move around at all I would need to help him get about. Three other men were terribly injured. One who had been unconscious for several days but recently come round was mentally not with us. Another had just had his lower leg amputated, and there was a Catholic priest who was paralysed from the waist down.

The next morning, we discovered that one had died. The more able men buried him under a pile of rocks. The officer and a few of the others discussed plans. Clearly, DP and some others weren't fit to move at all. We were only a few miles to the north of Suvla beach, yet we were unsure who would or would not make it. Where could the less strong men go for shelter until help could be sent?

As the day passed, a party of three men went out, returning an hour later. They'd found a farmhouse on top of the cliffs and reckoned that if we could get everyone there, we could shelter, rest and wait for them to send help.

So, we all headed up the cliffs, very slowly in the case of a couple of the patients, and we made it to the farmhouse. It had been deserted, but was perfect for us to stay in for a few days. There were matches and some logs, which we all agreed were the most important things, as well as some oranges and jam and a few other scraps of food. Dr Sheridan had been pressured to stay with us by the officer despite arguing that he would be needed back at the Clearing Station. It was so typical of the man to try to wheedle his way out of a difficult situation.

Prissie joked that he would be of greater use to the Turks wherever he was, and all the men laughed.

The officer said that they had to go, as it was daylight, and decided that it would be best if they weren't armed. They thought it would be safer to be in a Red Cross situation, rather than a military one. So, he passed his pistol and some bullets across to us and hoped we wouldn't need to use them.

They promised to send help as soon as they could and off they went: a snake of green, with the four sailors in blue, each fit man supporting an injured one. The officer was at the front with a stick, and on it a white handkerchief. It was a tragic sight, and we wondered if they had any chance. If the Turks didn't get them, then the weather surely would.

Dr Sheridan kept out of our way. It would have been much better if he had gone with the others the day before. He was by now in no doubt how much I disliked and mistrusted him, and I was convinced he would disappear at the first sign of trouble.

That night he checked DP's dressings. I was shocked when DP asked for a word with him. Reluctantly, Dr Sheridan agreed. DP encouraged him to go, stressing that he was needed more on the front line or with the rest of the patients at Suvla. He reassured the doctor that Prissie and I would look after him.

Dr Sheridan responded in a voice that was filled with insinuation: 'Oh, Louise will look after you, all right.'

With that, I slapped him hard. There was a stunned silence for a second and he rushed out of the farmhouse. Prissie came in to find me shouting, 'I'll kill him! I'll kill him! I will!'

I could see how tense DP was. I knew he wanted to defend me and sensed his frustration that he could not. 'Just wait till he comes back,' he said. 'I'll give him a piece of my mind!'

But Dr Sheridan didn't reappear until late that night. I stood in the shadows, close to the bed, listening to the fire crackling. He sat down on the bed beside DP. I don't think he knew I was there.

He told DP that he was leaving, that he was going to follow the same route as the others along the coast. DP said nothing. Then I heard the doctor whispering to DP that I had had it in for him since we were on the ship coming out and that he couldn't stay.

DP replied. 'You're right. You should go. None of us trusts you, or likes you. Louise is right, and if I were able, I'd kill you. You're a charlatan, and it's only a matter of time before you're exposed.'

Dr Sheridan was speechless. When we woke the next morning, there was no sign of him. The scraps of food we had to keep us going were also missing.

Chapter 7

WAR

Along with the two nurses and us injured is a very young officer, Mr Skinner. He was knocked out as the beetle was being loaded and only regained consciousness yesterday. He was left with us to command our party – perhaps there was concern whether he would be up to the trip.

With the majority of the fit and able men gone, we are left wondering how long it will take them to send a rescue party for us. They may already have emerged behind the Turkish trenches, and been captured. We will definitely be here for a few days; any longer will be a problem as we'll run out of food. Although we hadn't heard formally from our officers, the allied forces seem to be planning a retreat from Gallipoli. There were a lot of rumours among those in the Casualty Station that early December would be the date for complete withdrawal.

The nurses have got everyone here organised. Louise made up beds in the main living area so that we could make the most of the fire. Helped by Mr Skinner, they dragged a couple of mattresses down, then went off again and came back with armfuls of straw and wood from the stable.

We are stripped down to our underwear and our clothes are hanging up to dry.

'Does it hurt as bad, DP?' Louise asks me. She prods my wound gently with her finger. 'It looks all right. At least it's not septic.'

She unwraps the bandage around my head, bathes my eyes with water and dabs the seepage off with a cloth. I can feel her breath on my cheek and the warmth of her body only inches from mine. When Dr Sheridan treated my eyes he hurt me, but with Louise it is as if she is caressing me.

'Your left isn't too great,' she says, 'but the right doesn't look too bad now. I can see the green of your eye, and it definitely reacts to the light when I open your eyelid. Let's leave the bandage off tonight and you can exercise the muscles. Keep opening it and try to hold it open.'

I nod. Over the next hour, I do this and can definitely see light – even the comforting flicker of the fire! I feel so excited, so pleased with this improvement, that I'm convinced it's going to get better and better over the days ahead. I tell everyone, and both Louise and Prissie come over to exclaim and ruffle my hair, sharing my excitement.

Wrapped in blankets and with a roaring fire, we are soon comfortable. Food is the only real issue; the oranges and coffee won't last long. Prissie and Louise search high and low and come up with some flour, forgotten in a pantry. They manage to bake something – a cross between bread and a biscuit – and serve it with jam. It is a real saviour.

'I hope the others are all right,' says Prissie. 'It's so cold outside.' Those are the last words I hear before I doze off.

*

'It's stopped snowing!' Louise exclaims next morning. 'I hope the Turks don't come down here. Maybe we should hang a white sheet on a stick.'

My eye is getting better. It is wet and gooey, but after it has been bathed and I open and shut my eyelids for a minute, there is definite improvement. I can make out the shape of people and see them moving around, and also the location of the door and window.

We talk about how long it might take for a rescue party to come and find us; we reckon at least two days. Will they come by boat, or along the shore? We hope it will be by boat as then they would take us straight to the *Gloucester Castle*.

'What will we do if they don't come?' I venture.

No one has an answer.

'Come on, DP,' says Louise. 'We need to get you more comfortable walking around. We need to build your strength up, too.'

'I'll need a *cromach*,' I say.

'A what?'

I grin. 'A *cromach* is a stick that we take to the hill when we're working the sheep, or for balance. I'll need a dog, too. A Highland man always has to have a dog with him. But a *cromach* for now and we'll get the dog later.'

Louise finds a stick and we go outside. Carefully, she puts her arm across my shoulder and shows me how to sweep the stick back and forth to detect obstacles, to lift my feet higher rather than shuffle, and to bend and straighten my injured arm. 'We'll do this all day, DP,' she says. 'You need to be a lot fitter than this.'

As we stand together in the warm evening sun it seems difficult to imagine the dreadful weather of just two days before. I gently flex my arm, and Louise rubs the muscle when I get spasms and cramps. I can see shapes and movement quite well, but no colour yet, and everything is blurred. Louise has made a patch for my left eye.

'You look quite rakish, DP! It suits you,' Prissie exclaims. 'I can almost see some naughtiness in you now. Not the perfect DP we thought you were.'

'Are you tired of my stories?' I ask Louise, somewhat belatedly. 'They must mean nothing to you. A distant people in a faraway land.'

I feel her move close to me. 'They're lovely, DP,' she replies. 'What a wonderful life you and your family have had. I long to see it for myself.'

I think I believe her. I feel happy. I inhale her scent and control the urge to touch her cheek. I want to so much. I could kiss her right now. No one would see. But I don't; she might run inside. If only I could see her eyes; then I could tell what she is thinking.

There's a shout from Prissie. 'Come on, Louise! We have lots to do before the light fades.'

The other three patients are in as incapable a state as myself. The priest, Father Joseph, lies in the bed beside me.

I speak to him. His speech is slurred, as if he has been drinking. He'd been hit by shrapnel in the back and brought in by a party from HQ who were returning from a recce at the front.

Then there is the sapper corporal who lost a leg on a mine. Although it has been amputated above the knee, the stump has gone gangrenous, and the stench is awful. Prissie says it is like sharing a room with a man long dead. Back in the Casualty Station, Dr Sheridan had put the stump in boiling water to try and kill the infection. He also strapped on a bag of maggots to eat the rotting flesh. The poor man has an awful fever and screams terribly in his delirium, for hour upon hour. I ask Louise if he could be moved to another part of the house as no one can rest with the noise of his suffering. He will be dead by the morning, I think. God bless him.

Louise tells me that Prissie has something of a soft spot for officers. Mr Skinner and I talk a lot. He came straight from officer training at Mons and had been on the way up to join his battalion in the west. He was staying overnight with a rearguard party on the beach when they were shelled and he was knocked out. He is keen to get back to join them, and is worried that we think he is malingering. His father is a lawyer and he is desperate to go to university and become a lawyer, too.

His privileged life is as different from ours as you can imagine, but nothing is too much effort for him. He dashes about, collecting wood for the fire and carrying things eagerly for the nurses. Louise tells me that Prissie takes his pulse constantly and feels his brow, and we laugh. Prissie always has a good story to tell. She keeps everyone in good humour, especially Mr Skinner.

The sapper does, indeed, die in the night. Mr Skinner helps Prissie and Louise carry him outside where they pile stones over him and mark his grave with a little wooden cross. Back in the house, Father Joseph says a prayer for him and asks him to have a word with our maker when he arrives up above to see if He can get us out of here. It is a selfish thing to think, but it is so good to have silence again. His constant moaning was distressing, and put all of us on edge.

Several days pass. Prissie and Louise find a couple of chickens which Mr Skinner kills and plucks. They boil them over the fire. We are growing increasingly worried: why haven't we been rescued? Prissie and Louise are looking at all the alternatives to get to safety. Maybe the evacuation is over, and everyone has gone? But we all agree that it couldn't have happened that quickly. I am privately concerned about how I am going to get around: the disorientation and vulnerability that I'd felt when stumbling out of the beetle and onto the rocks the other day is fresh in my mind. I had fallen repeatedly, the waves soaking me up to the waist, and cracked my shin several times. Without a sailor on each side I would never have made it. Just walking for a few minutes exhausts me, still.

Mr Skinner gives us a map which he had with him. It turns out to be crucial. At the time, we hadn't even considered retreating overland, but this map gives us another alternative if our troops have indeed been evacuated.

As part of his officers' course at Mons, Skinner was taught about escape and evasion. He tells us that the choice is whether to look like locals and act normally, which carries the risk of being shot as spies, or to stay in uniform, move at night and be soldiers attempting to get back home, in which case we would be taken as prisoners of war. We know that, with two women, there is a decent chance we can pass as locals from a distance, so that is the option we have chosen.

Mr Skinner traces a finger over the map, showing the nurses a possible route. 'Basically, you need to head north for a week of steady walking to the neck of the Gallipoli peninsula, then another couple of days towards the town of Kesan. From there, you turn west towards Ipsala and the border for about a week, and after you cross the river Evros you're in Bulgaria. Another few days' walking to Alexandroupolis, and you should be able to get a boat to safety – Greece, maybe.'

My heart sinks. They all know that even half an hour's walking is difficult enough for me.

'A month of walking through rough country?' Louise says. 'How on earth will you manage, DP?'

'Well, it'll be a challenge,' I reply. 'But we have no choice.'

We know that the river that forms the boundary between Turkey and Bulgaria will be extremely difficult to cross. But Skinner says that there are many people in that part of Turkey and Bulgaria who are of Greek origin and Christian; we might find someone who would help us get a boat across.

And so we have the beginnings of a plan. Louise and Prissie spend many hours with Skinner discussing alternative routes. I sleep a lot, but I overhear Skinner explaining how we must avoid roads yet always read the road signs, and how local women will be much more amenable to help than men. Despite this advice, avoiding people at all costs seems to be the message.

Today, we hear distant shelling. The wind is coming from the south, so clearly the engagement is still on. I think about the poor buggers at the front. They'll be curled up in trenches scraped out of impossibly hard ground, the scream of shells headed in their direction above them, followed by the thud as they hit the ground. There was nothing they could do to defend themselves – the shell either has your name on it, or it hasn't. And they would be cold. While it is much warmer and the snow is nearly gone, the men would be soaked through and freezing, especially at night. It is strange to feel so fortunate.

We need a horse and cart, if possible. With the sapper dead and Mr Skinner heading off shortly, only the priest and myself remain among the patients.

The following day, Mr Skinner announces that he'll be leaving tomorrow, first thing. He's going to head along the bottom of the cliff face and hope that no one will see him. He does one great favour before he leaves. Taking the pistol, he goes out and shoots a goat. He skins and guts it, before chopping it into manageable pieces. I stand beside him as he does it and tell him where to cut. I've done it often enough with hinds and sheep alongside my father, though I am in no fit state to be of any use to Skinner at the moment.

We have a word before he goes.

'I'm leaving you some money, and I'll send someone back to get you,' he says. 'I promise. But if they don't come within three days you'll need to head off yourselves. Every day you're here is a worry. We aren't that far from the front line. If neither the main party, Dr Sheridan nor I have sent a rescue party it will be because we've been captured . . . or something.'

Prissie accompanies him for the first mile and climbs up the hill to see the fleet. On her return, she rushes into the house, crying, 'I've seen a donkey! We must go and get it. We can move DP around on it.'

Louise finds some rope, and between us we make a basic halter. I know how to make one, of course, but my arm and eyesight are still next to useless and explaining it isn't easy. They don't have much call for halters in the Welsh Valleys or Liverpool.

The women go out to look for the animal, but despite searching for hours they can't find it.

*

I have a good conversation with Father Joseph. He can talk only very little, and nod his head in response. I can tell he is in real pain.

Brought up in Liverpool, he had converted to Catholicism a few years ago and went to work in Ireland, teaching for a religious order. He became a priest only recently. He didn't know of my brother, though they must have been about the same age. We have a good rapport, given the circumstances.

Father Joseph was assigned to join the Royal Green Jackets, which was a regiment largely made up of soldiers of Irish descent. But not long after getting off the ship, he was hit by shrapnel and paralysed.

He is acutely aware of the problem. Prissie, Louise and I are able to walk; he is not. There is a reasonable chance of our reaching safety, with only the nurses and myself moving at night, but although he is a small man, we can't carry him. If we leave him here he won't be capable of looking after himself, and being a Christian priest he is not likely to be treated well by the Muslim Turks, who after all, are fighting a religious war. It is an agonising dilemma for us all.

*

Over the last two years there have been terrible stories circulating about the Turks massacring three quarters of a million Armenians: men, women and children. The Armenians are Christian, and moved down from Russia over the centuries and settled here. Whenever someone said that the Turks played a clean war by not shooting at our stretcher bearers or hospital ships, Colonel Willie would say, 'Remember the Armenians'.

'I'll bet this house was owned by Armenians,' I say. 'That would explain why the cupboards have food in them, and their clothes are still here.'

'You have to leave me here,' insists Father Joseph. 'I'll be fine. The Lord is at my side.' If he hadn't been a priest we would have left him the pistol to shoot himself with if he'd had to.

*

It is now close to Christmas. The weather is pretty rotten. At least we have the shelter of the house and wood to burn, unlike the poor sods in their trenches. Two weeks have gone by, and there is no sign of anyone. Prissie and Louise take it in turn to go to the top of the hill and look at the ships offshore. They tell me that the *Gloucester Castle* is there, looking white and beautiful.

'Must be at least six miles away,' reckons Prissie. 'With all those ravines I don't think we'd get you there, even if there weren't Turkish troops in the way.'

We have a lengthy discussion about what to do. Six miles is nothing compared to a month's walk to the port, but the terrain is very rough, and no one has succeeded in sending help for us. We can only conclude that they didn't make it through. If they couldn't make it, what chance do we have?

'I just feel we have no chance of getting to Suvla,' Louise says at last. 'At least heading away from the battle we can lie up during the day and sneak our way through in our own time.'

We all agree. This is our plan.

We decide to wait two more days, to see if anyone comes. Maybe the weather will improve, too. We hear distant gunfire, but see no one.

I am definitely getting stronger. My shoulder is stiff and painful, but I know it is on the mend. I am not looking forward to stumbling across rough ground, but Louise keeps me at my exercises, half an hour four times a day. We practise climbing fences and fallen trees, even running, though that is a disaster. On the odd sunny day, Louise and I walk around the steading. She pushes me to walk up hills and down steep slopes to get me used to exertion. I ask her to tell me about the flowers and the trees, as I still find it impossible to make out any detail, but she doesn't know any of them.

'A mining town in Wales wasn't the place to learn about these things,' she says, with a grin.

I can move around the steading now, and walk for about an hour before I need a rest. My eyes are sore but not infected. I wear a hat taken from the farmhouse to stop the glare of the winter sun.

Prissie is drying out pieces of goat meat in front of the fire, and Louise is filling wine gourds with water for the trip, when we hear a horse approach. We hide in the farmhouse until we are sure it is an ally, and then we greet the man warmly.

He introduces himself. 'I'm a New Zealander, from the Otago Mounted Rifles. John Stewart.'

He tells us that he had been sent to do reconnaissance and had been unable to get back to his regiment on Hill One Hundred with news, as there were Turks between him and his unit. He hasn't eaten for days, so Prissie gives him some of the precious goat.

He was trying to get to Suvla and had tried from various angles. It seemed that there were Turks everywhere and our troops were trying to get off the beaches and onto the boats as quickly as possible, loading at night so the Turks didn't know of the evacuation. Like all Aussies and New Zealanders I have encountered, he is friendly and open; we all warm to him.

I ask him if he had come across a Dr Sheridan on the way. He had not, but he had seen a man with a donkey in the distance, which might have been him.

'Our donkey, probably. I hope the Turks get him,' says Prissie.

Nor had he news of the sailors and injured who left two weeks ago. He promises to get a message to the Scouts to let them know how we are, if he possibly can.

We have decided to leave tomorrow. We are sitting in the main room, shivering in the cold and covered with blankets. John is adamant that we won't get back to the beach along the shore. The others from our beetle may have managed, but the path has Turks positioned all along its length. He has decided to head around to the east and have another crack at it. We discuss our route – exactly the opposite way from where our troops were getting loaded onto boats on Suvla Bay. But we can't stay here. The Turkish troops are sure to come, and what with Sandy and I having suffered so gruesomely at their hands already, I am not keen to rely on their decency.

Father Joe doesn't join our conversation. We are all acutely aware that he is not coming. There is no point in discussing it.

Louise and Prissie go through every drawer and cupboard, digging out clothes for us.

'How do I look?' jokes Louise, posing for Prissie in a large straw hat.

Prissie tosses a woollen coat in her direction. 'Goes well with this jacket – quite the rage!'

They try on various items, and I can hear that John is enjoying the show. 'The less you have on, the better I like it, ladies,' he says.

I feel a twinge of jealousy.

Me in an army uniform and them in their scarlet nurses' uniform is not going to be a sensible way to play it. We need to be the colour of the ground and the bushes, as we intend to travel at night and take shelter during the day. The women who sell the cigarettes on the beach wear black and brown clothing, with a shawl over their heads. Of course, the problem is that the menfolk who had lived in this house were a great deal shorter and more stocky than me. I am not far off six foot and very slim. There are heavy leather sandals with a strap that we can adjust for our bigger feet, however. We won't pass muster under scrutiny, but from a hundred yards away we might get away with it.

As we sit by the fire, sipping some ouzo, which we had found hidden with the owners' clothing, we try not to think about the journey ahead.

'Tell us a story, DP,' pleads Prissie. 'Cheer us up. Louise tells me you spent some time making whisky. Tell us about that.'

'Ach, that story will take hours, and I really need to sleep. Have I told you about the clipping of the sheep, though?'

HOME

As my father explained to me, sheep were quite new in the Highlands and had been the reason for some of the Clearances, which saw tens of thousands of people thrown out of their crofts. After the 1745 rebellion, a lot of the clan chiefs fled to France to escape persecution. Over the next fifty years they broke their link with their people and they spent serious money. They moved from being fathers of the clan to being masters of the clan in their own mind – a subtle but significant shift. The chiefs now needed their vast acres of unproductive land to support them. In many instances, their people were moved, forcibly driven in some instances, from productive to barren land in order that professional shepherds and thousands of sheep could be installed in their place.

It hadn't been that serious an issue around Lochaber, although Clanranald had sold almost all their land in the last hundred years to finance their gambling and high living in the south. In fact, that was how Ardnish came to be owned by the Astley-Nicholsons and Inverailort by the Cameron-Heads.

Anyway, each year at the start of the summer everyone around got involved in the clipping. We would meet at an early hour and have a cup of tea and a bowl of porridge. Each of the men heading off on the gathering would have several collies scampering around.

The hill would be divided up by my mother: 'Donald Angus, you go up the Alt Ruar burn, and where it peters out at the top, cut up past the trees and bring all the sheep from there to where the big boulder hangs over the cliff, back to the fank. Donald Auch, you go with him, but at the top, go over and do the other side of the hill.'

It seemed that everyone in the area was called Macdonald or Gillies, and what is more, most were called Donald as a first name. So they were given a second name, and maybe also a name of where they lived. For example, my father was Donald Peter Auch – *achadh* being a field in Gaelic

– because he had the grazing of the big field behind Peanmeanach. You could also be known after your job: Allan the whaler became known simply as 'the whaler' because he used to go off on the whaling boats.

So, half a dozen men and a few youngsters would head off, with maybe twenty dogs loping along behind their masters. It was quite a sight. They would cover maybe a dozen miles before they were home; big strides across the rough hillside, with never a pause for a breath. Every man was fit. They never once looked at the rough ground as they strode across it. I didn't notice this until I'd been away, but the Highland shepherd is always looking at his dogs or his sheep, never where his feet are about to go.

Johnny, 'the Bochan', was well known in the area. An old man now, he had never married and had seventeen collies. He never missed Sunday Mass, walking five miles each way to see the priest.

Just behind the Polish church was a shed, about the size of an outside toilet. He would cram all the collies in – with the last two or three picked up by the scruff of their necks and dropped in on top of the others – turn the latch on the door and go in for Mass. One time, a couple of visitors came by and, hearing whining and snuffling from the privy, unhooked the door. The sheepdogs came tumbling out and ran straight through the front door of the church and up the aisle to find their master.

He was well known for his love of a dram, very friendly and good with the *craic* on visits, frequently staying until he was swept out of the house at dawn. My father said that everyone he drank with had a head as sore as can be the next day, but the Bochan was never affected. Many a girl had set their eye on him, my mother said, but he was happy in his croft at the end of Ardnish peninsula, with its beautiful views of the sunsets over the Small Isles. He had a wee boat to catch a fish or two, and was always available to help with gathering.

As the sun fell towards the west and smoke rose from the village fires, the sheep would begin to arrive in the village. A couple of hundred here, and the same again from the west. There was a fenced-in bit of lowland, known as 'the park', and 1,600 ewes and lambs would be there for the night. We would get to our beds early, as the next day would be the busiest of the year.

We were up before daylight, and you wouldn't believe the noise of the bleating and plaintive cries when we separated the lambs from their mothers.

After our early shift, we went in for a big breakfast, with the men being joined by my Macdonald cousins from Laggan, two fourteen-year-old twins from over the hill. Kirsty McAlastair and her father rowed across from Glenuig, setting off at four in the morning.

Not just a gathering of sheep, it was a gathering of the people. It tied the communities together, introduced the young to one another, and brought important money into the village in the form of pay from the estate. This week it was Ardnish; next week it was Meoble; and the following Glenuig. We all helped each other.

We would be given different jobs. The most important was the clipping, where three men sat on triangular stools and wielded twelve-inch-long scissors, which they sharpened on a piece of sandstone. The wit was sharp, too. 'Damn it, Archie, get your son on that stool. You're too old to make yourself a cup of tea, never mind wrestle with an Ardnish ewe.' Or, 'Watch it, Bochan. That ewe will have herself in your bed by the end of the night, the way she's looking at you.'

Then there were three who went into the fank and took a ewe each by the horns and pulled her towards the clippers. When the stool was empty, she was twisted onto her back in a very inelegant way, legs pedalling like fury. The clipper would start at the neck and clip down between the skin and the wool. The Bochan was the undisputed champion; it took him only a couple of minutes, and he never drew blood as he deftly moved his clippers back and forth. He could clip all day without a sore back; everyone else had to take it in turns.

The others did a variety of jobs. That day, Kirsty and I took the fleece and rolled it into a ball, twisting it this way and that, and pulling a bit through that we could use to bind the bundle together. There was a knack to it. The fleece would then be chucked across to those packing it into the hessian bale. As a bonus, there was always a chance for a wee bit of flirting with me knocking the fleece out of Kirsty's hand as she was finishing, or a nudge off-balance as she threw the wool up to Sandy.

My father shouted at me, 'Boy, will you get on with the job and stop mucking about,' as the others would remind him that he might just have done the same thing when he was a lad himself. The bale was hung from a ten-foot goal post, and Sandy would jump up and down to pack the wool in. He knew to make sure the top few fleeces were nice and clean, as the wool buyer from Lancashire would open the bag and look at the quality before be bought it.

Tea would be brought along by my mother, a piece would be eaten, and usually we would be finished by darkness. That day, there were fourteen of us working together. It was a beautiful day I'll always remember.

My mother told us that Jemima Blackburn used to get rowed across from Roshven House to paint everyone at the clipping, sometimes with a couple of friends. She would come if it was dry and there was a breeze to keep the midges away, an easel would be set up out of the way on the bank, looking down into the fank where the men and sheep were working. She was well liked. The Bochan would shout up – in English, of course – 'Make sure you don't make my nose too big in that painting of yours, Mrs B,' or my father would be asking what percentage of the royalties the men would get if she sold the painting. The *craic* was always good at the clipping. The Astley-Nicholsons' factor came across to see how we were doing, too, with half a case of whisky for us for that night. Sometimes Sir Arthur and Lady Gertrude rode across, and we would have to speak in English (those of us who spoke it). The Bochan had a collie called Arthur, and he'd shout, 'Arthur, Arthur! Come away and lie down!' which disconcerted the laird somewhat and made us children giggle with delight.

Exhausted though everyone was after two long hard days, with aching backs from all the bending over as we handled the shears, and wet though from the drenching we'd endured after lunch, everyone agreed it had gone well. We had mutton stew that night, having received permission from the factor for a sheep to be slaughtered. Quite a few drams were taken and stories about the old days told, then Sandy, fired up by the whisky, suggested a swim. Soon, the five of us younger ones were pelting across the machair and into the sea. We tore up the seaweed and covered our heads in it, and took it in turns to dive off the rocks while our families kept an eye on us from the house.

And that's my story of the clipping of the sheep . . .

WAR

John, who has been quiet throughout my tale, speaks up: 'It's just like our place back in Dunedin. It's all about the sheep, the water – even the people have the same names. I didn't think there were any of you left in the old country, thought they'd all moved to New Zealand.' He sighs. 'Anyway, I'll be heading off first thing. Please don't get up. I'll get my own breakfast. It's been lovely to meet you all, and good luck getting out of here. I'll be sure to tell the Poms where you are if I can.'

We all shake hands, sorry to see him go.

'Time for bed,' says Prissie, and the others leave Father Joseph and me alone.

'You tell a good story, DP. Where did you learn that from?' he murmurs.

'It's just the way in the West Highlands, Father. Everyone sits in the front room, the neighbours come by, you will have seven-year-olds and seventy-year-olds around the fire, there will be tea or a dram in the hand, and the stories of the ancestors are told back and forth. My father will have told me stories of two hundred years ago, which are as fresh as when his great-grandfather told his grandfather. It's the same with poems and songs – we're brought up with them.'

The priest and I talk late into the night. He is very weak now, and I feel he may just slip off to our maker as soon as we depart. He tells me he has lost a lot of blood. I even wonder, briefly, if I should give him the last rites. I don't, and I later regret it. It is good to talk to him; I know he enjoyed hearing about my family and its strong faith. I take some comfort in the thought that he will pass on knowing he was with a friend to the end.

Chapter 8

WAR

Up at dawn. It is very quiet outside. The shelling in the distance has stopped. Hopefully, this means our lads have got off the beaches and are safely on the ships and heading home. John had told us that General Stopford, the overall commander, had been sacked and replaced. One of the worst campaigns in military history, he said. Certainly tens of thousands of dead men – and no ground won.

As we drink our coffee we discuss John; we all agree what a charming man he is.

'If I wasn't going to live in the Highlands I'd go to South Island,' I say. 'God's country, I hear. You can get good farm land for buttons, and Scots are welcomed with open arms.'

Prissie packs for each of us: a blanket twisted around some clothing, and as much food as we can carry. Louise conceals the pistol in her clothing. We are dressed in the drab peasant clothing of our absent hosts. Louise and Prissie wear shawls over their heads, trying to look like the old grandmothers from home. I am as strong as I have been for a month, but can only really move at half the pace of a normal man. How am I going to make it?

We say emotional farewells to Father Joseph, silently willing him to slip away before the Turks come. He is gracious, holding our hands and whispering a prayer to St Christopher, the patron saint of travellers.

'Thank you,' I whisper.

God, we will need it.

*

The plan is to head away from the battle lines and stick to the coastline. We reckon we have about twenty miles to go before we come to any towns or proper roads. Hopefully, our route won't be on the Turkish troops' supply lines. Talk is of the clear skies and sunshine. Hard crisp snow lies underfoot, perfect for making progress but bad for making our dark bodies distinct against the glaring white. It isn't too bad at first, but as I begin to tire, I catch a foot and fall awkwardly several times. And despite the bitter cold, I am in a terrible sweat which chills me to the bone whenever we stop moving.

We stick to the bottom of the glen, on a goat path through thick brush, which at least gives us some cover, though every twig that snaps under our feet makes us pause and listen.

After what seems an age, probably only an hour or so, Louise spots a hut and we rest. My legs are shaking violently, and I feel feverish. I sense Louise is worried about me. But we have to get some real distance between us and the front line; if the battle has really finished, there might be troops withdrawing our way.

We stay in the hut until late afternoon. I try to sleep a little. Then we are off again, to try and cover more ground. After a while the moon comes out, and it is a great help to me, as I stumble along, desperately hoping for another building to give us shelter for the night.

I start to experience vivid flashbacks: Sandy dying, my childhood. I cling to the recollection of Sandy. He is always in my thoughts. At times like this, he would have been the reassuring one, my rock of stability. I so much wanted him to meet Louise; his opinion of her would have meant the world to me. I am certain he would have loved her.

Louise and Prissie hold my hand in turns, and I do my best to keep moving at a steady pace. We end up lying against a wall, huddled against each other for warmth. But the night is awful. Our clothes are soaked with sweat which has frozen, and we are hungry. Every inch of my body hurts.

The next morning, Louise tells me I was crying out all night.

We can't light a fire, as we are still too close to possible troops, and farmers in the area would spot us. I feel hellish stiff from the night's cold. We shiver and shake until the sun rises.

And then, I hear Louise exclaim, 'A donkey! Over there by that barn.'

'Sssh,' Prissie warns, 'the farmer could be anywhere.'

We lie on the snow and wait. After a while, Prissie creeps forward and, seeing no footprints in the snow, urges Louise to join her. The donkey is apparently very hungry and is following Prissie around, hoping for food.

Louise has the halter that we made a couple of days ago. 'It's perfect,' she says, delighted at the change in our fortunes. The girls fuss around the animal, stroking its ears and patting him.

'He's so small and you're so tall, DP,' says Prissie. 'Your feet will be dragging along the ground, but you're all skin and bones, as light as a feather!'

I clamber on. Very uncomfortable it is, too, but we can move much more quickly now. Louise takes my *cromach* in one hand and the halter in the other. With her shawl over her head, I think how biblical the scene must look.

The donkey makes a huge difference to our speed, though its noisy hee-hawing is a concern.

Late afternoon, we reach the base of a cliff. It looms above us; according to Prissie, it must be about five hundred feet high. She scrambles a way up, to see if she can observe anything.

'Just goats and hares,' she says on her return. We plod on.

After an uncomfortable hour or so, Louise spots a building and goes to investigate. To our delight, it turns out to be a derelict farm, hidden from the main track which skirts the mountain, nestling in a hollow.

'Even a fire would be invisible here,' Prissie beams, as we make our way towards it.

We lead the donkey inside, and feed it hay from an outbuilding. Already, this was promising to be a much better night than the one before.

The fire is wonderful. We chew contentedly at our dried goat meat and stare into the flames.

'What shall we call your donkey?' says Prissie. 'I know. What's the word for donkey in Gaelic?'

I explain that we don't have a word for donkey as we don't have any donkeys, just as we don't have a word for camels . . . They giggle.

'If he was a horse we'd call him *marc-shluagh*. Marc means warhorse.'

'Perfect! Marc it is,' declares Louise.

As we huddle around the fire, Louise nudges me gently. 'It's going to be a long night, DP. I think we need another story. Tell us about your sister . . .'

HOME

Sheena emigrated to Mabou, Cape Breton, in Canada about four years ago. When her Angus was drowned off Smirisary she had a terrible year. Her carefully planned life was destroyed, and she had begun to feel as though she didn't really fit in, that her life had no purpose. Mother was great with her, keeping her busy, but at tea-time Sheena would just sit quietly. She had always been such a lot of fun, collecting gunpowder from father's gun to make bangers that made everyone jump at ceilidhs, or, famously, putting a goat in the room of a drunken man who'd made advances to her. It was sad to see her spark gone.

Emigration had been a big thing at home. From about 1840 there had been a steady trickle of people leaving, mainly due to the land not being able to support the population, with the potato crop failing and a cholera outbreak.

Father Rankin had set up berths for ships to Australia, and over 500 had gone from Moidart alone.

My father always said it was the kelp boom that created the problem: the population had doubled on the west coast. Then that collapsed and there was a huge demand for sheep's wool, so the lairds wanted the cattle off and sheep on. That was all very well, but sheep need far fewer people to handle them. So, you had people with no kelp money and no cattle of their own, and the laird employing just the odd one or two shepherds, rather than the many men who had been required before. Then the price of wool and mutton fell, too, and the estates became deer forests, often for English industrialists.

Years ago, Ardnish had four real settlements, and 200 folk lived on the peninsula. It's now down to about thirty, scattered here and there. Of these, only two have regular jobs: John MacEachan, the postman, and John Macdonald, a shepherd at Laggan. A bit of fishing and shellfish collecting, a bit of money from gathering and clipping the sheep, and other piecemeal work done for the laird, a hind or two taken when the factor wasn't looking, and, of course, money sent back from the family who had left for Glasgow or further afield – that was how we managed. The old and the sick died of starvation, really. Every house had rent to pay, and finding actual money wasn't easy, but luckily our laird would allow us to build walls or do other casual work in lieu of rent.

The people from Ardnish tended to go to the east coast of Canada – Nova Scotia, New Brunswick or Prince Edward Island. It was often the priests who organised the boats. It was a voluntary thing in our part of the Highlands, though once news started coming back of the free land given to settlers, the moose to eat, furs to trap and sell to the Hudson Bay Company, good housing and plentiful wood, there was a rush, even though the winters were harder than ours. And one thing the people there really knew about was how to endure a long hard winter.

Macdonald of Glenaladale went from Glenfinnan, and sent news back inviting people to join him. And almost all of them did. He came back once, and it rained for every second of his stay. He was heard later to say, 'I can see why my people left.'

*

Sheena left one spring day. She heard a boat was due to go, and travelled to Fort William to buy a one-way ticket.

Our parents were desperately sad but they knew she needed a change. Glasgow was rough with the dirt and the fighting, not to mention the cramped slums and danger of disease. Besides, we were never going to be city people. We had family in Cape Breton who would have her to stay. They spoke our language, they played the fiddle and the pipes, and they worked the land. Maybe, my parents hoped, there would be a good man for Sheena to marry.

She knew a few of those going in the boat. There were Campbells from as far as Oban, MacNeils and Macleans from the islands of Barra and Tiree, and a good number of Macdonalds from Brae Roy and areas around Fort William.

The boat would stop at South Uist to gather another fifty people.

We went to the Fort to see her off. My God, how distraught people were at the quay. Many were men heading off to see how it was before they sent for their families; their wives would know a thing or two about hunger before things got better. Young families were saying farewell to aged parents who had decided to stay in the glens they were part of. The tickets were expensive, and most passengers had borrowed at an awful cost to buy them.

'The promised land had better be bountiful,' my mother said. She was determined to be brave, and we were all given a firm lecture before we headed off on the train.

Sheena has sent letters since, of course, urging us to go out and promising us that she would come back. I couldn't see either happening myself. She had a job working for a big family of nine children, helping the mother with the children and teaching them to read and write. Mother said she would be good at that. She lived on the shore, where Iain MacNeill, her employer, and a cousin of our grandmother, had a fishing boat. He was a terribly hard worker, she wrote. Away before dawn, and then with two other men he would be offshore for two nights before coming back. The catch was huge, but the prices were low. She liked the family a great deal. She spoke of the lovely hot summers, the glorious colours of the trees in the autumn, and winters so cold that a night outside would kill a man. Sometimes the sea froze so solid you could walk between islands, miles out to sea. She wrote of the ceilidhs in Glencoe Hall and the incredible musical tradition, how

Gaelic was the language of everyone and Catholicism the only religion. It sounded just the same as our Lochaber. There were bear and moose, she wrote, and the land was covered in trees as far as you could see in every direction. Everyone was very poor, though, and feeding the family and the animals through the winter was as much as the people could achieve – and that only just.

Mother was dying to hear if she had a man in her life – she always said Sheena would make a great wife to the right man – but to her frustration, we knew the last thing Sheena would do would be to mention this sort of thing in her letters. She had always been like that, discreet and not one to raise expectations.

WAR

We are heading to the town of Kesan and from there towards Greece and the allies. How we get back to Britain is something we'll worry about later, but with Louise, Prissie and now Marc on my side I feel I have a chance.

Marc is a Godsend. Placid and obliging, he ambles behind the women, snatching at any leafy branch or patch of grass that catches his eye. I can visualise the donkey by the crypt at the Polnish church at Christmas. Marc seems to know how fragile I am; he is undoubtedly my saviour now.

Mr Skinner had told us that just before the war Bulgaria had seized a strip of land from Greece that bordered the Mediterranean, so technically we will be crossing from enemy country to enemy country. We wonder if the people still consider themselves Greek and if they have sided with the enemy Bulgars, but we don't know. We shall have to tread carefully.

The terrain is one of rolling hills in barren land with brush, like hawthorn, about six feet high. It is excellent cover, but we are aware that the first we might see of soldiers would be if we walk right into them. From time to time we walk through pine trees. The excellent path must be used by villagers moving along the coast, which is a concern, but we have no option. The undergrowth would be impossible to get through.

The biggest physical obstacle is going to be the river Evros – the former boundary of Greece, now Bulgaria, and Turkey – and how to cross it. But before we reach it, and before Kesan, lies a narrow neck of land at the top of Gallipoli. The map shows the road running along the top of the peninsula and a big river. We might need to go along the road at this point. Between us and the border would be many troops, and as we get further from the battle there would be more civilians around, some of whom might be more than happy to turn us in.

Prissie had gone off half an hour ahead of us to check that the way ahead was clear. If she doesn't reappear soon, we are to turn around and meet back at the farm. She has the pistol so she can fire a warning shot if need be.

At one stage, she came running back and we had to push the donkey into the brush and hide while a farmer with a laden mule passed by. Since then, we have made good progress and we are now well clear of the mountain. We must be twenty miles from the battle line. We know the people around here will have had little to do with the war, which has never really encroached inland, so we hope they will be less hostile towards us should we encounter them.

My right eye is making a great recovery, still very sore in the morning with pus hardening to make a crust, but Louise bathes it and after a few minutes of blinking I can see tolerably well. Not good enough to read a book or discern colours, but I can see shapes and movement, and beautiful Louise. My left eye is a disaster; there seems to be no chance of recovery. We keep it bandaged.

Today is Christmas Day. We agree to do a short day if we can find somewhere safe to hide, and our luck is in. We come upon a shepherd's hut on the hillside, well protected by trees. Prissie ties the rope around the donkey's feet to stop him straying. A small fire is lit, and we make ourselves comfortable for the night. We eat the very last of our meagre provisions; it's not much of a Christmas feast.

'What would your family be doing today?' Prissie asks.

'Go on, tell us,' urges Louise . . .

HOME

Well, Christmas five years ago would be very special, as in those days Sheena and Angus were there. There would be Mass at the beautiful church of Polnish, so after an early breakfast we would set off on the two-hour walk, Father on his garron, us walking, with everyone from Ardnish going the same way. Maybe fifty in total. The folk from the other communities would appear as we got closer. 'Mary Anne, how lovely to be seeing you, and, Colin, still alive are you? Is that old mare I gave you still with us?'

Everyone would be dressed in their Sunday best, with frocks for the women and the odd man wearing his old army kilt. The children would be spoilt: 'Here's a penny for you, Donald Peter. Go and buy yourself some sweets when you get a chance. And Happy Christmas to you, you're a fine young man now and no mistake about it.'

Mass was said by Father Allan Campbell, and being Christmas Day and taking pity on the wee ones, it was over and done with in an hour and a half. The way back was a bit of a race; all the young were dying to get back to see what presents had been bought. Even though the adults would take much longer and have to put the dinner in the oven, there was no holding us back. I got a *cromach* that my father had made for me: a lovely straight shaft and a tup's horn top, soaked and worked into the shape of an 'N', with 'DP' carved and blackened on one side and the Macdonald of Clanranald crest carved on the other. I could not have been more proud of it. My father got up very early for a month to work secretly on it. Angus got a bamboo fishing rod and Sheena a beautiful jumper knitted by our mother.

Eilidh, the old lady from next door, came to join us, bringing a bottle of illegal whisky she had been hiding these last fifteen years as a present.

After presents was lunch. Food was normally never plentiful at the house, but compared to those in the city it was bountiful. Baked eggs, followed by a fine haunch of venison that the laird had delivered to all those who had helped over the stalking season. Mother had grown turnips and potatoes, and we had rhubarb and gooseberry fool to finish with. All this was washed down with the whisky, even I as a fifteen-year-old boy was allowed some. A bit of fiddling and piping of Christmas carols, and the neighbours would come around to tell stories as we all sat around the fire. It was lovely.

WAR

Louise is silent.

I look at her. 'What about you, Louise? Tell me about your Christmas.'

She doesn't answer, and I can tell she is crying.

Eventually she says, 'We had nothing like that, DP. We didn't look forward to Christmas at all.' She pokes the fire a bit, and nothing more is said.

Prissie doesn't tell us about her Christmas in Liverpool, and we don't ask.

*

There is hardly any food left, and nothing to be foraged. The ground is rock hard with frost. We need to find more, or we stand no chance of survival, so Louise and Prissie decide to go out the next day to see if they can beg some scraps from farmers in the area. And if that doesn't work, Prissie swears she'll use the pistol. One way or another, they will get something.

They are in luck. Within half an hour's foray from our base, they come across a farm that is occupied. Hens are scratching around outside, and it looks normal, even though there is a full-scale war on twenty miles or so away.

Even with my poor vision, I can discern the red-tiled roofs and once white walls of the farmhouse and the outbuildings.

We move back so Marc doesn't raise the alarm, and Louise and Prissie leave me leaning against a tree while they creep forward. They are away for what seems a very long time.

Later they tell me that they saw two older women going about their domestic duties, collecting wood for the fire and feeding a large dog that was tied outside.

To avoid surprising the dog, they went back and around to the side of the house and then rushed the place – Prissie to the front and Louise to the back – to stop the old women escaping. I would love to have seen it. By then the dog was barking and straining at its rope. With Prissie waving the pistol at them, the women swiftly surrendered – they obviously had a higher opinion than I did of Prissie's ability to actually use it. Within minutes, the two captives were trying to win their intruders over by offering tea, though Prissie didn't drop her guard with her pistol.

Louise came back to fetch me, recounting the adventure as she led me to the farmhouse. The minute the old women saw me with my injured eyes and struggling gait, they understood, though Louise pointing at me and saying 'bang-bang' definitely helped.

We put the donkey in a shed with theirs and give it something to eat. Louise and one of the Turkish women make some food for us. I swear the chicken stew is the best food I've had since I've left my mother's kitchen. Louise and Prissie take it in turns to hold the pistol at the ready while the other eats. There isn't a word the two women say that we can understand and vice versa, but they seem to have decided that we won't hurt them and that if they look after us we will soon be gone. We guess they are sisters. We never learn their names.

*

Almost everything tastes different from what I have grown up with; for instance I had never had coffee before we landed in Gallipoli. There are no chillies or olives at home; even pepper is new to me. Louise thought this was amusing. She loved watching me grimace as I drank my coffee, yet before long I was drinking as much as they can give me. The Turks add a lot of goats' milk and a couple of spoons of honey; I like mine black and bitter. The bread is more like a hard pancake, which they have with honey in the morning. Olives are served with everything, though I get Louise to take these off my fork – they are not for me. In the stew, there are all sorts of herbs that are very tasty, and the wine is strong and sweet. I drink too much of it and try to explain to the sisters, in Gaelic, about my family and my home. Having been on army rations and having had almost no alcohol since Egypt, we are in a very strange sort of heaven.

I even sing a song to the four of them, while hiccupping violently. I suspect the old women haven't been entertained like this before.

In our family we always say grace before we eat, and I am pleased that Louise has started saying this with me. Prissie thinks God is a lot of nonsense, but she doesn't start eating until Louise and I have prayed. Our prayer seems to have an effect upon the *cailleachs*. Louise tells me they have crucifixes and statues of the Virgin Mary in the house. We wonder if they have heard of the massacres – maybe they have lost their families?

My eyes are dry and itchy, although there is no longer any sign of infection. Louise boils water, washes the dressings and bathes my eyes. I am still very weak and underweight. There is a lot of discussion about why this could be, and what could be done. I confess I enjoy the attention, fancying maybe that Louise takes longer than she needs to attend to me.

I am shown to the only bedroom. Louise and Prissie take it in turns to sit in the kitchen with the sisters. There are two soft chairs and the sisters sleep fitfully in those, while Louise or Prissie perch uncomfortably on a stool against a wall, trying hard not to fall asleep.

We stay for two days, eat as much food as they give us, and recover our strength. We feel a little guilty, but if anyone is as untouched by war as these two *cailleachs* in the whole of Europe, they would be hard to find. While one sister goes about the work of the farm, watched by Louise, the other is kept hostage in the kitchen by Prissie.

By lunchtime of the second day we decide we trust them, the gun is put away, and that night everyone sleeps soundly. Snow falls overnight, and there is an inch on the ground when we awake. It is beautiful, with all the trees coated and glistening in the weak sunshine, and complete silence outside.

There are about twenty goats and lots of hens, and there is an olive grove and some vines. Prior to our departure,

Louise and Prissie cook up some extra food and, with the help of one of the sisters, make some bread. We pack some dried goat meat to keep us going for another three days. The dogs they use to herd the goats are twice the size of our collies at home, big, hairy and powerful. I can imagine them fighting off predators such as bears in the old days. Louise tells me that the goats are every colour under the sun: pure white, light brown and a combination of black, brown and white.

As Christmases behind enemy lines go, we could scarcely have done better. We worry at first that the *cailleachs* will immediately rush off to tell the authorities about us and a search party will ensue, but despite our gun and our intrusion we feel they are on our side. They have no reason to be loyal to the Muslims.

We say a strange stilted farewell, with Prissie trying to give them some of the money that Mr Skinner had given us. They refuse to take it. Instead, they take our hands in theirs and say what appears to be a heartfelt goodbye. Nevertheless, we head off in the wrong direction then make a big loop around the farm to take the correct direction. We can't take any chances at this stage.

Prissie thinks we are nearing the road. Hopefully, we'll come across a sign telling us where we are and how far we have to go. Any village will do. The temperature is rising, the snow has melted, our donkey is most co-operative, and we are as cheerful as we can be. But, as we travel further from the farm, the brush gets more and more sparse and our anxiety grows. We realise we must be visible for miles around.

We can see the sea in the distance on our left and the hills to the north on our right. The road is a real concern. We watch hundreds of horses pulling wagons and guns, and a stream of soldiers. We retreat into the cover of the brush a couple of miles from the road and head up the peninsula parallel to the road for the rest of the day. Prissie carries her pistol and moves ahead of us at all times.

And then, we get the fright of our lives. Prissie is running back, shouting, 'Quick, quick, hide!'

Before we can get out of the way, a man appears in front of us with a rifle in his hands, pointing it and shouting at Prissie. They are just feet away from each other. Prissie has her pistol pointed at him, holding it with both hands, yet still he shouts and advances.

Louise and I cower together, expecting him to shoot at any time. I can feel her shaking like a leaf beside me. We stare helplessly at the stranger.

There is a huge bang of gunfire, followed by silence, and then a shriek.

'Oh my God, my God!' Prissie cries, the pistol dangling from her hand. 'It went off by mistake, I was shaking so much. I didn't mean to kill him!'

We gather to look down at the man lying on his back. Blood is oozing from an open wound in his chest, his face registering the shock of the last moments of his life. Prissie's accidental shot has hit him right through the heart. Underneath the tangle of his hair is an unlined youthful face.

'He's a boy, just a boy!' sobs Prissie as she clings to me. 'Oh God, how I hate this war!'

Louise puts an arm around her and strokes her hair. 'There was nothing else we could do,' she soothes.

We need to hide him. And so, without another word, we drag the dead man by his feet down the hill and out of sight. Finally, keen to get away, we move off quickly. Nobody talks for a good hour as we try to come to terms with what has just happened. My admiration for Prissie grows. Without her swift action, we would surely all be lying dead by now.

Towards the end of the day we find ourselves on a rise, looking down onto a vast plain, absolutely flat, maybe five miles across: the neck of the Gallipoli peninsula. A large deep river divides it in two with a single bridge for the road. This will be our most dangerous time. We lie on a grassy knoll, watching the Turkish soldiers heading north towards Constantinople.

'What a shambles they are,' scoffs Prissie. 'They look just like armed peasants.'

'Well, they beat a hundred thousand of our finest men,' I reply.

I can swim, but neither Prissie nor Louise can, and getting Marc across the river is likely to be impossible. Louise decides to go down to the river and see if there are any crossing points. In the evening light, Prissie watches her, hunched over like an old woman, making her way slowly down to the river and along its bank, two hundred yards away and in full view of a thousand Turkish troops. There are some goats grazing down there; hopefully they'll assume they belong to her.

I can only sit, tense with fear, and pray for her safe return.

She comes back just as it is growing dark, mud up to her knees, with the news that the road bridge is the only way across.

'The river is wide and deep, and very muddy along the banks,' she says. 'There's no way we can get across. All the locals must use the road bridge.'

What can we do? We decide to rest up and gather our thoughts. Lying head to head, we talk about Prissie's shot.

'My first murder,' she says, her voice heavy with horror. 'What if he was just coming to offer us food?'

'He had a gun, and it was pointed at us. You did the right thing, Prissie. We would be dead now, or worse – handed across to the Turkish army,' I say, trying to sound as reassuring as possible. 'People bringing you supper don't threaten you with guns.'

'Still, though, I'll never forget the look on his face when he was hit,' Prissie whispers.

We chew on our goat meat, and lie shivering in the cold in silence. We would have to cross the bridge at night, and head into the hills beyond where the peninsula ended and the land stretched to the town of Kesan, and then west. We might only be thirty miles from the border now.

Under a full moon, we set off towards the road. It's a big risk, but what would be the point in delaying? The chaos of the war might mean that there is a gap between the groups of soldiers along the route and we can slip through, unobserved. Will our donkey alert everyone, or will the horses along the road stamp and whinny as we approach?

We wait about three hundred yards from the road while Louise crawls forward to see if there is an opportunity. Prissie and I sit in a hollow, wrapped up in our blankets, shivering. If there are any alert sentries they might challenge us, but with the battle lost and everyone homeward bound we can't believe local peasants would be of much interest to them.

Louise comes back. She's had trouble finding us again. 'Everyone is lying asleep by the road,' she whispers. 'They might wake up, but we've got a chance of passing through quickly. We must go now, though. I don't think it's going to be safer any other time.'

I am helped up onto Marc. My stomach is churning with fear as we approach. We seem to be making a hell of a noise. Marc is snapping every twig underfoot, although luckily he's not braying. The worst thing is, I can see next to nothing; my wretched eyes are useless in the gloom. How close are we? Is anyone stirring? Is that a soldier lifting his gun? I have to trust to fate.

The donkey lurches up a bank, and I hang on tightly. I can hear Turkish horses snickering at our arrival and there are fires glowing dimly all along the road far into the distance. We go along a hard road for a few minutes, before dropping down the other side. Once again I feel the long grasses against my legs.

We've made it.

I have never been so nervous in my life. Sweat is pouring off me. An agonising twenty minutes later, we stop and I am helped off the donkey. For a few moments, we all hold each other for support. Louise starts laughing – sheer relief after all the anxiety. We are all trembling. We must have been only a few feet away from men who were sleeping and we seemed to have made a din like an army charging, but we have got away with it.

'I could definitely hear men talking, really close by,' says Prissie. 'If one near us had woken we would have had a hundred of them all around us in seconds.'

We head closer to the sea and keep moving along the plain, parallel to the road, for a couple of miles. We push through an overgrown path, grasses up to our chest. We are now a good mile away from the Turkish troops.

By mid morning we arrive in the foothills and settle down to rest, camping down by the sea in a little inlet. Offshore are two very striking islands; even with my vision I can see their outline, like two whales, a mother and calf. Listening to the murmuring of the sea and the cries of the seabirds reminds me of home. We feel safe here. We can't be seen from the hills above or from the road. It is almost warm as Louise and I lie together, almost touching.

I drift off to sleep and wake to see her looking very intently at me. She looks guilty, like a child caught stealing a biscuit. I smile; she smiles.

We risk a fire that evening, collecting dry driftwood along the shore so that there is minimal smoke. As the birds wheel about and call, I talk about the birds at Ardnish . . .

HOME

My mother always talked about wildlife, but it is birds she likes the most. She and Mrs Blackburn sometimes went on bird-spotting trips together; they came to Canna to see puffins when I was working out there. There are eagles at Meoble, and along the shore of Loch Shiel, we once went up and saw an eyrie when Mother was there doing the lambing. They fly over Peanmeanach and get mobbed by the hoodie crows. On the beach, there are flocks of dunlins which run back and forth in time with the waves; they are incredibly endearing. Then we have terns, lots of gulls, some eider duck and even some corncrake that live in the big field behind the village. And there is a cormorant that sits like an old black widow on a rock on the beach. My mother has Mrs Blackburn's book of bird paintings and she shows us which is which.

WAR

We reckon we are more than halfway to the border. We wake early, untether the donkey and set off, in heavily scented pine woods now. But the weather is deteriorating. Cold, unrelenting rain soaks us through. Our woollen clothes grow heavier, and we are feeling utterly miserable. We all know we will become sick if we spend the night out in this.

We battle on for a few hours, before admitting defeat and taking shelter under a big rock for most of the day. We don't speak, just watch the water pouring down the flanks of our donkey as it stands with its ears flattened and head down. In the evening, we head off again, Prissie ahead of us. We are not as cautious as before.

Prissie dashes back to tell us she has seen candlelight in a window. We whisper a plan of action. We have to do the same as the last time and hope that the result will be as successful. I am left on the donkey so that if all goes wrong they can come running back and we can escape into the darkness. As it happens, it is just a sweet old man who sits nodding as we set up camp around him. His house is in a dreadful state; I can see through the roof in some places and there is a bare earthen floor with puddles. There is only one room with a raised bed in the corner, a table and stool. Within half an hour, we have our wet clothes steaming by a roaring fire and the girls are cooking some of our chicken. We share it with the old man who is most grateful. He doesn't seem to have any food in the house at all. He must be ninety years old at least, and he is as deaf as a post.

Chapter 9

WAR

We talk into the early hours, huddled round the fire in scratchy and no doubt flea-infested blankets, as the old man snores quietly.

Although Prissie doesn't have the lovely singsong voice of the Welsh Valleys that Louise has, it took me a while to gather that she was from Liverpool. Having had so little to do with people from outwith the West Highlands I struggle to guess where people are from. I persuade her to tell me a bit about herself.

Louise and I lean against each other and listen as her story unfolds . . .

PRISSIE

My father was a docker at the Albert Docks in Liverpool. He was a big strong man and made a good wage loading and unloading the huge freight ships that came and went from the empire. Liverpool was a great place to work. It was said that forty per cent of the world's trade went through the dockyards there. The pay was good, and there were always treats that came our way from loads that were spilled – the dockers would squirrel some away to take home. For instance, I'd had a pineapple years before any of my friends, and even bananas arrived on our table a couple of times a year.

Liverpool Docks had thousands of working men, and when the horn blasted for shift changes, the crowds pouring up the road and into the town were amazing to see. They were all men, all wearing hats, all smoking, and all wearing black or brown, dirty and tired from carrying big loads to and from the ships. Lugging sacks of coal for twelve hours a day was hard work.

When my sisters, Colleen and Caitlin, and I were young, there was always a gap somewhere in the fence that went around the docks that we could slip through at night. We'd wander around, and now again the Port police would give us a hell of a fright. We'd end up sprinting around the boxes and bales being chased by huge men wielding sticks. My parents were furious when Caitlin let slip one day where we had been, and we were made to promise not to go through the wire again. 'Your dad will lose his job if they find out!' my mother said.

The place was intoxicating. We were in awe of the Cunard and White Star liners, on which the rich would head off to New York or Argentina. Then there were the grain ships leaving and the meat loads arriving. Horses pulling carts, the steam and whistles of the trains as they pushed and pulled loads across the docks. The men were all colours – coolies from China and blacks from Africa

– and it was all part of the excitement and wonder of the place.

Because Dad's job was important for the war effort he didn't get called up to fight, and because of the war our family prospered. There were fewer men available to work, and the supply ships that set off for Gallipoli and other places of war tended to go from Liverpool.

Dad was fanatical about football and used to go and watch Everton every Saturday afternoon, even taking the train to Manchester or Blackburn. He was a good man. He didn't drink too much, never laid a hand on Mother, and made good money.

My parents were lucky to get good jobs. Being Catholic, Mother would avoid any conversation about religion. 'If anyone at school calls you a Fenian *teag* or anything like that, ignore them, and don't get into a fight.'

There had been a bad time last year, though. Dad was guiding a big bale of cotton that had come from America onto the dock. Three men were feeding the rope through the block-and-tackle when one of them slipped. The rope ripped through his hands and the bale landed heavily on Dad. He broke his arm, the bone sticking through the skin. He was in agony.

There were so many injuries at the docks that they had their own doctors, and within the hour they had given him some morphine, reset the bone, bandaged it up, and sent him home. There were few places in England where you would be sorted as well as that. He did have ten weeks on no pay, though, which was difficult, though luckily my parents had some savings put away in the building society.

My mother was a matron in the Liverpool Royal Infirmary, which was said to be the best in the world. She loved her job and went off to work each day in her starched and spotless uniform. We were terribly proud of her. I was always going to be a nurse, from my earliest days. Sometimes she would work nights and sometimes a day shift, so with both parents away we girls had the run of the city. By God, she was strict, though, and if we hadn't done our school work or our daily chores, we got a thrashing from Dad when he came home.

Because Mum and Dad both had good jobs, we had a comfortable life and lived in a good house in a nice area. My sister Colleen was very clever. She read all day and loved going to school. Her teacher came to Mum one day when Colleen was thirteen and said that there was a chance she could get to university. She could apply to the Blue Coat School, which had just moved to new buildings out of town. It was set up for orphans, but they had some vacancies and she could sleep there during the week.

At first, Colleen didn't want to go, but Mum came up with the idea that she could try and study to be a doctor – one of the first female doctors! Florence Nightingale had come from near our home, so anything to do with medicine was a big thing for all the girls in our house. Anyway, she sat the exams and got in; there was great excitement. Both Caitlin and I were quite jealous, but we were proud, too. The Blue Coat children were very obvious in the city centre as they wore such old-fashioned clothing.

Despite the prosperity of Liverpool, there had been terrible unrest in the years coming up to the war. The city was sucking in people, many from Ireland like our family who had come for work. The old people from the city resented the Catholic flood and created areas that we weren't allowed to live in. Men would be beaten and women would fight like vixens. On Thursday nights, the men would be given their pay, and the women would be at the gates of the docks where they would meet the men, take the pay packet and give some of it back so they could go down to the pub. Late that night, the wife would go down and find her man and lead him unsteadily back to the house; some had it easier than others.

There were some ports that wouldn't employ Catholics, and there was even the stoning of the Catholic bishop's carriage by a handful of ruffians a few years ago. This coincided with a number of strikes that brought the ports to a halt, and the army was called in. It became known as Bloody Sunday, when strikers were killed by police. A gunboat was even sent to the Mersey.

I wanted to get away. A Scouser I will always be, but I don't want to live there. When recruitment for the war was in full flow, I took my chance.

Mum told me about the Queen Alexandra nurses. Quite a few were trained in Liverpool, and she knew one of their matrons a bit, so we had her round for tea. She arrived in her beautiful uniform, with a scarlet cape that only the officers wore. She spoke about the travel to distant countries, how the soldiers were so grateful for the help, and what fun all the nurses had together. Before the war, there were less than 300 of us, and we had to be over twenty-five, but she explained that there was now a huge recruitment drive – they were keen to have another 2,000 nurses as soon as possible.

Mum was so flustered before she came. Everything was scrubbed and polished, and fancy cakes were baked. 'She's very posh,' she warned us, 'but very nice, too.'

I finished school in June, and within a month I had been for my interview. A week later, I was offered a place on their training course. There were great celebrations in our house – the neighbours all came round and so did my schoolfriends. I showed them pictures in the recruitment flyers of the scarlet-and-grey uniforms and the white hats like nuns they wore. Everyone was very impressed, and my mum was especially proud of me.

So I headed off down to the outskirts of London, to a big red-brick military hospital, with a wing that was set aside for our training and accommodation, and found myself in the bed beside my now best friend – Louise.

WAR

I bombard Prissie with questions. Does she have a boyfriend? Did she do well at school? Had she had fights with Protestants herself? But it seems she has told us all she is prepared to, for the time being.

Louise piles more of the wood onto the fire and we eventually doze off. We are lying in smelly old blankets on hard ground, but it is bliss being sheltered from the rain and wind outside.

After a terrible sleep we pull on our damp clothes. Louise gets the fire going and Prissie puts water on for coffee. After a week of travelling, I badly need a wash and a shave.

I sit in my underwear with a bowl of hot water and a cloth and try to give myself a wash, but when I twist my shoulder it stings. Louise sits beside me and, without saying a word, takes the cloth. In complete silence, she moves the cloth all over my body; it feels like a declaration of devotion. Not a word is said. Her breathing and my heart pounding. I now know for certain she feels the same about me. As she wipes my face, she doesn't catch my eye. I can see that she is blushing ... Despite my pain and the cold, I smile like a contented cat.

We aim to reach the outskirts of Kesan – maybe ten or fifteen miles away, we guess. The little donkey is quickly becoming a good friend. I must be a heavy load, despite being so underweight, and he has eaten little since we left, although we always try to find him grazing when we stop.

Animals can sense things. Sea birds come inland before a big storm, for example. I heard of a man whose dog barked and barked and kept pulling a man away from under a big tree in a storm. He was just out of the way when there was a crack and a huge branch came down just where he had been standing. Maybe Marc is aware of my incapacity and senses I need help.

We are startled when two children come around a bend. They say something, and we smile and wave our hands in a friendly greeting. They run past us. We're fairly sure they'll just think of us as strangers passing through the area. They look like children in the Highlands: smiling faces, well-darned clothes, barefoot. Maybe they're off to school. Fortunately, the weather is getting better. We decide to rest behind a wall for a while, eating the last of the bread and honey and soaking up the sun.

Louise and Prissie can see smoke from the town of Kesan a couple of miles away. There is a stretch of flat land in between, with little cover for us. The town has a mosque in the middle. There are people in the surrounding fields herding sheep and goats and heading into town with laden pack animals. We know there is a large army camp on the outskirts, but we haven't seen any patrols. They clearly believe that the battle has been won and they are not in danger. We have no intention of getting any closer to the Turkish army than we have to, though.

As we skirt around the town we notice a signpost on the road to Ipsala, which is the main border crossing. It is about thirty miles away, so maybe four days' travelling at our gentle pace. We decide to risk moving a bit faster by going along the road early in the morning and resting up during the day. Because the area is so flat, we have at least a mile of good visibility and warning of other people. We are feeling a bit more confident now. We no longer expect to encounter armed men behind every bush.

Louise and Prissie up the pace and take it in turns to pull the donkey, who reluctantly breaks into an ungainly trot. It is me who slows the pace, as it is a constant strain to grip with my legs. We pass some old men with mules, but no words are spoken.

Taking cover in the middle of the day, we talk about the river crossing. Everything depends on this and it has come to dominate our conversation of late.

We near a small village, and, as usual, survey it from a distance. Prissie spots a cross in the main square. Could the people there be Christian? She decides to go into the village. 'I look the most like the locals,' she says. 'My dark hair will help, as long as I don't open my mouth and reveal my Scouse accent.'

Wrapping herself up, she heads off to see if there is food for sale.

Louise and I make ourselves comfortable, and talk about what it might be like across the border and if we will be able to find help in getting us home. We touch on our wishes for later life – everything, really, apart from my love for her. It is always on my lips, but I never quite find the moment. I curse myself for not speaking to her about my feelings, but maybe it is for the best. We need to concentrate on our immediate predicament.

It is Louise who realises that our disappearance might trigger a 'missing' telegram to our families. Maybe it would read 'missing – presumed dead'. How long did these things take, we wondered. Our families would be distraught.

We are getting hungry now, and we are worried about Prissie. Louise loosens my dressing and bathes my eyes. It is a month or so since they were burned. I can only just see the blurred town in the distance, but, best of all, I can see Louise's features clearly. My shoulder has mended to a large extent, and I don't wear the sling any more.

We doze off in companionable silence, leaning against each other for warmth. I awake with my head on her lap, my hand around her legs. We don't say anything. I blush and move my hand away. She takes it back and rests it on her thighs.

She moves into a kneeling position and kisses me. My heart is going like a train. After a while, she leans into me and we talk for a long time.

We confess, at last, our love for each other. I tell her I've adored her from the first days in hospital, how when she passed my cot my hand would reach out to her. She tells me, to my astonishment, how we first met on the train in England, and that we are meant to be together.

Perhaps I'd known all along but hadn't let myself believe it. That beautiful singsong Welsh voice, the way my skin felt so alive whenever she was near. I'd felt it before. Of course she was the girl on the train! Ever since I had arrived at the casualty station, I'd been drawn to her, knowing that we were familiar to each other, that there was a connection. But I must have blanked out all reason. I suspect that the morphine had lent a sort of oblivion to my senses.

'I didn't know you cared, that you felt the same way.' Louise is sobbing gently on my shoulder. She covers my face with kisses. 'I was never sure. DP, I'm so glad you're here with me, despite everything.'

'Me, too,' I say. I feel euphoric.

*

Prissie still hasn't returned. It's pitch black. We are panicking a bit, but there is nothing we can do, except wait.

I pray that we all make it back to a safe country together. I wrestle briefly with my conscience, knowing that God would greatly disapprove of our intimacies, and offer up an apology, although I avoid any mention of not doing it again.

Where is Prissie? We fear she must have been captured or has been unable to find our hiding place.

'I'm going back to the road to see if I can find her,' Louise announces. 'I'll be no more than fifteen minutes, I promise.' She squeezes my hand and stands up to go, before bending down to give me one more long kiss.

She returns alone and, despite our worry, we fall asleep, intertwined like lovers, under a single blanket.

Chapter 10

WAR

It is mid morning and the winter sun is quite warm on us
when we hear someone coming through the bushes. The
donkey snorts and stamps around. We freeze, terrified,
until Prissie comes into view, a big smile on her face.

'God, Prissie, you scared us to death,' Louise exclaims.

Prissie excitedly takes the pack off her back and shows
us her haul: cheeses, meat, bread, some water, and even a
gourd of wine. We are ecstatic – and starving.

As we eat, Prissie tells us her story.

*

I walked, as bold and confident as I could manage, right into
the village square and stood in front of a Christian church.
The writing on it looked Greek rather than Turkish, which
gave me hope. Anyway, I then found a shop, but because of
the queue of women in there I decided to come back when it
was empty. I didn't want anyone to suspect that I was a
foreigner. So I went back to the empty church to wait. A priest
with a long beard was busying himself inside and after quite

a long time he came across. I was pretending to pray on my knees, looking down with my head bowed and hands together.

He sat beside me and waited, and after a minute or two it was clear that he wouldn't go until we had spoken. I looked him in the eye, and he knew I was not there to pray. He spoke to me, and of course I didn't understand a word he said. My throat was dry and I struggled to utter a word.

He smiled, and gestured for me to follow him. He took me into a room behind the altar. If it wasn't for his friendly way I would have run out of the church as fast as I could. He spoke English! I was so relieved I burst into tears.

It was incredible. Apparently he had been an Orthodox priest in London when he was young. He gave me some coffee, bread and cheese. He was Greek, and he thought that Greece would come out as an ally of the British. He had been expecting to be called back home at any time. He mentioned there were lots of Christians around here, and most of them consider themselves friends of the Greeks. The Muslim Turks had dragged many men away and killed them, and he'd expected his church to be burned down. The only thing saving them was the fact that the German generals who commanded the Turkish army were Christian, and ever since Gallipoli, the massacres have stopped.

I told him all about us. I said that our biggest concern was crossing the river into Bulgaria, and he said he would help. I could have kissed him.

It was getting dark. He said I wouldn't find my way back and asked me to stay. He said he'd get more food for all of us and to come back in the morning. I knew you'd be worried, but what an outcome!

He showed me to a cot in a small room and told me he was going out to talk to friends about our predicament. My first bed in a week, I slept like the dead. He woke me in the morning and over breakfast told me the son of a friend would lead us to a house in Ipsala. There, plans would be made to take us across the border. We would be in safe hands – the people were Greek Christians – and they would look after us.

He took my few drachmas and went out and bought far more than my money could have gained. Then he returned with a man who spoke no English, but was very friendly. He was with his son. The priest introduced the son as Dimitris. He's fourteen, and I had to go with him to agree where we would all meet. Meanwhile, the priest assured me our escape would be all arranged. I just clasped his hands in mine and kissed them, I couldn't thank him enough.

He looked me in the eye and said a prayer, and then made the sign of the cross over me. I may be a non-believer, but by God, this might make me reconsider.

Dimitris and I went out the back of the church and up the hill, not far from where we were hiding. The priest had agreed we would meet tomorrow in the middle of the day. Dimitris will whistle if the coast's clear.

I think we must be the luckiest people in the world!

*

We have a whole day to wait, but it's not too cold and we have eaten well. We agree to stay where we are and do without a fire until nightfall. I lie thinking about Louise and me, then about home and Father Angus. I hope he's not in danger; I never got a letter from him. Is he happy as a priest?

HOME

Angus always had that leaning. We had a wonderful priest at Polnish when we were young – Father Allan Macdonald, who had gone to serve in South Uist. Angus would serve as an altar boy, do the readings at Mass, and was always questioning father about transubstantiation and other issues.

My father hated those discussions. 'I'm Catholic because I'm Catholic, Angus. Go and talk to Father Allan if you want that kind of conversation.'

I felt the same as my father.

My mother would talk to Angus about it while my father decided that he really needed to go and brush up on a tune he'd been learning. Mother thought Sheena might go off and become a nun, after her man was killed. She had even gone and had a talk with Father Allan about it. He advised her against it. 'You're just running away from life, seeking somewhere to hide from your misery. It's not a calling from God, Sheena,' he said. 'If you still want to become a nun in a few years' time then I would be happy to talk to you again.'

And, of course, they never did.

WAR

Just after dawn, the whistle comes as planned. Prissie brings Dimitris back to us. The priest is with him. We are all introduced by a proud and delighted Prissie.

'There has been a change of plan,' the priest begins. 'You will have to wait a few more days. Certain people are away, and we need to prepare your route and inform the people who will meet you. There is an old building where you can take shelter and light a fire while you wait. It's away from the road, a safe place. Prissie, your friends will have to wait here and you come with Dimitris back into the town. Bring the donkey with you. It doesn't look well, so we need to get some food and water for it, before you leave. Your friend won't go far without it. Rest up, and we'll be back tomorrow.'

I can tell that Prissie is quite happy to leave us again due to the prospect of good food, a bath and a bed, and Louise and I are excited about being alone together, so we don't mind waiting.

As soon as they leave, we build up the fire, cook and eat the chicken, and wash it down with some sweet wine. Emboldened by the alcohol, we kiss and cuddle and murmur sweet nothings to each other. Ultimately, the privacy of a closed door and more than two months of restrained passion leads to hours of intense exploration and fulfilment. The pain from my shoulder vanishes with the fervour and excitement of the consummation of our love.

*

Prissie and our guide return at midday. Marc looks much happier, having eaten well and slept in a bed of straw. Louise and Prissie whisper and giggle together; I blush to think of what they might be saying.

We pack up and set off, navigating along winding tracks in the brush, moving quickly for several hours. Eventually, we reach a large house where the occupants are clearly expecting us. A friendly family of five, they are much better off than any of the people we have seen so far. The father is called Georgios; the mother is extremely shy, and we don't catch her name. Georgios puts wood on the fire while his wife makes a big bowl of meat stew and the three young children tend to Marc. I am worried about him; he is stumbling more and more, and is very weak.

Our new friends try to talk to us and we to them, but little is understood, so we turn in early, grateful for the comfortable beds.

The next morning, before our convivial hosts wave us off, we are given bread and coffee, as well as something that tastes very similar to sour cream in honey. We all feel invigorated and ready for the journey ahead.

Louise says 'Ipsala?' to Dimitris, and he nods and holds up his index finger, indicating that we might reach there today.

However, it soon becomes apparent that Marc is on his last legs and is slowing us down. Yesterday was too hard on him and several days with little water or food have taken their toll. At one point, Dimitris breaks off a tree branch and whacks the donkey's rump and Louise flies at him, shouting in protest. He gets the message. Marc is important to us. This is the first time I have seen Louise annoyed. It reminds me of my mother; animals mean a lot to her, too.

As darkness falls, Dimitris goes ahead to organise the night's stay. We are exhausted, but excited that tomorrow we might cross the river. He returns with a man who we can hardly see in the twilight, and we follow them to a spot overlooking the town. We can see lights flickering in windows and people moving around.

Dimitris is going to leave us here. I embrace him and thank him profusely for his help. Just a young lad, he has impressed me very much.

The man smokes, paces around and tries to talk to us, but eventually we all give up. We sit for hours without talking, shivering in the cold wind. When all the lights go out in the houses below us, the man motions to us to follow him, and we move into the silent village.

We are taken to a house where another man greets us. Without a word, he hands us a candle and leads us up to the attic, where there is a mattress and bedding on the floor. We fall asleep before our heads hit the pillow.

I wake first, my body hard against Louise. I savour her warmth and the tiny movements of her body as she breathes in her sleep. Tentatively, I slide my hands under the bedclothes and move them over her body. I touch her breasts gently, my heart pounding. I can tell she is awake now, as she turns towards me. We kiss, and I stroke her hair. I can hear Prissie's heavy rhythmic breathing just feet away from us; with her there my ambitions are going to remain unfulfilled.

Outside, the town is full of activity, with cries from people in the street, the creak of wagon wheels and the clop of hooves. I enjoy these sounds of human activity.

There is a creak on the staircase, and a timid woman appears with a tray of breakfast for us.

'Donald,' says Prissie, 'you're always moving your fingers. What are you doing?'

'It's an affliction all pipers have,' I reply. 'The bottom stalk of the bagpipes is called a chanter and my fingers are busy playing a tune. They have a mind of their own. I don't even know I'm doing it. It keeps them from stiffening up, and maybe it helps me remember tunes better.'

Louise interjects proudly, 'DP's a famous piper, Prissie. The soldiers on the train all said he was!'

I do miss my pipes. All my life I have played an hour or two a day. I am always humming tunes and trying to recall a difficult passage. I hope the Colonel is looking after them for me.

We are left to ourselves all day. That night, late, the man who came to collect us from Dimitris returns with a companion named Yannis. He is a professor at Athens University and speaks perfect English. He apologises for our having been left alone so long but explains that he has been away and has only just heard of our arrival.

The men have a bottle of wine with them, so we sit and drink and listen to the two of them talking. They are discussing what might be the best plan. We are aware that we are entirely at their mercy.

Yannis tells us that they need to get in touch with a man about five miles upriver. He owes Yannis a favour – and he has a boat. There is a bridge very close and a ford, but both are heavily guarded and you need papers to get through. It would be much better to take a boat, Yannis thinks, even though there would be patrols going up and down the shore. He would come with us for the crossing, and then when we were on the far shore he would leave us to it. The Bulgar army would be on the far side; the Turks were on this side.

'The other side of the river was Greek territory until three years ago,' Yannis explains. 'The people there hate the Bulgars, and they're terrified of them. They are Greek – nice people – but the Bulgars are thugs and bullies. They look for an opportunity to smash your house up, to rape your wife and daughter. There are traitors and spies everywhere. The locals will want to help you, but they won't. Too much risk.'

Yannis is very animated; he constantly waves his arms about and shouts. I wonder if I look as scared as I feel. I wonder if he is scared, too. He continues: 'The Bulgars have a mad king, Tsar Ferdinand. His wife is German. That's the problem. They are always at war, the Bulgarians. They have just had two Balkan wars, and three months ago they declared war on the German side. The people where you are going consider themselves Greek, but they're being conscripted into the Bulgar army. If Greece sides with the British, then you will have Greeks fighting against Greeks. The people aren't happy. They have no money now because, with the men away fighting, they are not getting the farming done. Also, why have they sided with the Turkish Muslims when they are Christians like the Greeks and us? Their soldiers won't like that. There is a strong underground movement, I hear, but we don't have any connections with them.'

Louise and Prissie stare at him, becoming increasingly anxious. We know the political situation now, but it doesn't really make any difference.

'The British have men training them. Maybe you will be lucky and meet them. If I were you, I'd go to the port of Alexandroupolis. The Bulgars call it Dedeagach. There will fishing boats there, maybe there will be boats going to the Greek islands. Have you any money? You will have to pay the boatman.'

'We don't have any left,' admits Prissie. 'We used the last we had to buy food.'

'I think I know someone who might have some Greek money,' says Yannis. 'I'll go and ask later.'

He teaches us words in Greek that we will need: words for food, boat, please, thank you, bread, water, fire, hello, goodbye and 'we have no money'. He tells us about the kind of money they use across the border. We sit in a row repeating everything ten times each; it's just like learning Latin at school.

*

The next morning, we are out of the town before light, heading deep into the countryside. We stay away from the river. We are fearful, but encouraged that we know our destination and we have a plan.

At one point, Yannis and the other man leave us in a small steading and go off to find us some money. We eat bread and cheese and, to while away the time, I tell Louise and Prissie about the big hill fire that happened when I was about ten.

HOME

It was Aggie from next door who came to the house in the middle of the night. Fire was a constant worry to everyone. She said she could smell smoke, and sure enough, so could we. We all went outside to see where it was coming from.

'From the east,' said my father. 'Maybe the heather is burning.'

It had been dry for weeks. The steam train threw off sparks from its coal boiler; last year's dead bracken was lit very easily. There wasn't much we could do, save move the horses and cattle and our best possessions down onto the beach. We prepared some wet rags to cover our faces, just in case. By dawn we could see the glow of flames on the skyline.

'It'll be at Laggan within an hour or two. Angus, will you run along and see if they are all right? Come straight back though, and keep along the shore,' my father told him. 'It will be here by midday, so let's help the others clear their houses.'

In those days, there were maybe half a dozen fit strong men in the clachan, and they were soon carrying beds and other pieces of furniture down to the safety of the rocky shore. Animals were rounded up and herded to the shore, too. If they had panicked, there was little we could have done. The men were most concerned about the big field behind the house; if the hay was burned, there wouldn't be feed for the winter. So they headed off with rakes, spades and saws to try and make a space that the fire couldn't cross from the hillside to the field.

Father stayed with the families; with his leg he was no use.

'We need to say a prayer for the wind to drop,' said Mother. 'This is a real threat to the village. If the hay goes, families will have to leave.'

We knelt down and she led us. 'Hail Mary, full of grace . . .'

It was late that night when we knew we were all right. The men returned with blackened faces, exhausted. They had been beating out every flare-up, and the wind had switched to a northerly. We were safe. The men all went down and swam naked in the sea. They were heroes. We hoped that the people at Feorlindhu and Polnish were safe, too.

This is the worry of Peanmeanach now – none of those men left in the village. Sandy and I were the only two, and now even poor Sandy has gone. If that fire happened today, the hay would be burned, the animals would perish and the houses might burn down, too.

WAR

It is nightfall when the men return.

'It is a difficult situation,' Yannis explains. 'The boatman said there were too many patrols around and if he was caught they would shoot not only him, but his family. The only way it can work is if you steal the boat and row it across yourselves. If you make it, the boatman can retrieve it later. If you get caught, at least he can claim not to have been involved. But, my friends, there is some good news! I have some drachma for you. It's a decent amount that will allow you to buy enough food for a couple of weeks. So, you can leave tonight, or tomorrow. It's up to you.'

The news about the boat is not reassuring, but stealing it is our only option. We decide that we might as well go tonight. Every day we wait, we are in danger of getting caught and we worry about our kind rescuers being tortured and killed, too.

The boatman's house is a fifteen-minute walk away. His family are gone and there is no light. I pat Marc farewell and bury my head in his mane. Without him, we would never have made it much beyond the first couple of days. Prissie and Louise make a fuss of him, too. We take off his rope halter and take it with us; we might need it again on the other side as I will need to be carried over the longer distances. We leave him eating contentedly on the river bank.

The boat is down by the water. Louise helps me to clamber in. I sit in the front. Prissie tells us that she rowed a bit in Liverpool in her youth so she takes the oars. There is a whispered thanks to Yannis and his companion as they push us off.

The current takes a hold and we move quickly. Prissie noisily splashes the oars more than is comfortable, and my heart is racing as I strain to hear any cries from the shore. I can't see a thing in the pitch dark.

Then, with a gentle bump we are on the other side. We scramble out of the boat and collapse on the bank, laughing and laughing, giddy with the exhilaration of our adventure. We are getting closer to freedom . . .

Louise takes my hand and leads me into the darkness.

We come to a road junction where a sign reads 'DEDEAGACH 57 KM'. Yannis had said that was where we should be heading. We need a place to lie up for the day. We've had such generous help from the Christians in Turkey – how will things fare for us from here on?

I limp along, with Louise holding me by the hand. It feels good. I am in awe of the way she compensates for my poor eyes. With her I step out confidently.

We bed down under a clump of bushes, down a track away from the road. Yannis's wife has given us a bag crammed full of dates, cheese, bread and dried meat. But we are too tired to eat.

I wake first, with both girls lying sound asleep against me. I don't want to move. Neither my shoulder nor my eyes are sore, for the first time really. But I know I'm not a strong man any more. It has been seven or eight weeks since I was tortured. What a lot has happened since then. I imagine the evacuation has taken place. Did they get away from the peninsula without too many being killed? Where are the Lovat Scouts right now? Back in Egypt, maybe? Colonel Willie had been evacuated with dysentery, like Lord Lovat. I think of my fellow soldiers often. I picture Sandy. Where are you now, my friend? He'd be fishing, given half a chance, with a beer beside him.

'Pray for us, Sandy,' I whisper. 'There are dangerous times ahead.'

Aunt Mairi will have received notification that her son has been 'killed in action'; this not two years after her husband drowned. And no other children, either. I remember a story about all three brothers of the same family being killed in one attack. Unimaginable. Poor Aunt Mairi. She has my mother to care for her and is probably walking to Mass every day in Polnish, but she must think the Lord is punishing her, poor woman.

Louise says there are hospitals all over the Mediterranean now – on Lemnos and Malta, of course, at least a dozen in Alexandria, and even one in Gibraltar. They must be overflowing with Gallipoli patients. Three are for dysentery sufferers and for those needing operations. There are separate hospitals for officers, as well as convalescence hospitals. And the Anzacs, French and others all have their own. I wonder if we'll make it to one . . .

Louise wakes and stretches. We lie in silence, with her caressing the back of my neck.

We decide to stay here all day, with no fire. We have food, and Louise wants me to rest and rebuild my strength. They can go out and see what is going on now and again; two young girls will be less conspicuous than an injured man with a bandaged eye. We talk about the last few weeks and how lucky we have been. My God, the kind people we have met, and the little donkey. When we were hungry, there was always someone who had food for us. The weather has been less cold, too. We touch wood and pray our luck continues.

Prissie sets off to reconnoitre. 'I'll go and see if there's a path we can take rather than going along the road,' she says. 'Otherwise, we'll have to move at night. Maybe we can find another donkey.' She picks up the rope halter. 'If the going's good, we might manage seven miles a night. What do you reckon, DP? Think you can manage?'

I shake my head. I feel so useless.

We are on the edge of a marsh. After Prissie has gone, Louise goes for a quick look around. 'It's flat round here,' she reports. 'I think we're close to the sea – maybe a delta for the River Evros.'

At midday Louise tells me she feels hot and wants to vomit.

I hold my hand to her forehead; it is covered in sweat. She definitely has a temperature.

As the day wears on, she gets worse and worse, constantly rushing off with bouts of diarrhoea. I feel completely helpless. And scared.

By the time Prissie comes back, Louise is in a very bad way indeed. She has a terrible headache and delirium.

'It looks like dysentery,' Prissie says. 'Did she drink any dirty water?'

'She went off and came back saying there was a swamp,' I reply.

Louise whispers that she did drink some water, and that she is so sorry.

'I hope it's not cholera,' Prissie says quietly. 'Let's see in the morning. For now, we need clean water. She needs to drink lots.'

Prissie had seen a fast-flowing burn the night before, further along the bank. She picks up our gourd and sets off into the darkness.

'I hope I can find my way back,' she says. 'If not, it will be at first light. Look after her, DP.'

Louise thrashes around, dripping in sweat and making no sense. I am the nurse this time, but there's not much I can do except cradle her head in my arms and wipe the sweat from her brow.

Prissie returns in a couple of hours, with fresh water. She forces Louise to drink. 'Open wide, drink more . . . more,' she says. 'We'll need to find a doctor. We need medicine. There are a couple of places nearby I'll try.'

Louise is aware of Prissie's words and tells her how brave she is.

'Not at all,' Prissie replies. 'I just hunch myself over with my shawl round my neck and walk really slowly. I look like a sixty-year-old peasant off to do my shopping. I'll go to Peplos first, then Ferres. I'll be back as quick as I can.'

Louise is no longer delirious, thanks to all the clean water Prissie has poured into her, but she still has awful vomiting and diarrhoea. I help her as best I can.

'I'm sorry, DP,' she says again and again. 'It's so embarrassing.'

'Not at all, Louise,' I soothe. 'Every man in the battalion had it.'

'Talk to me,' she urges. 'Keep talking to me. I need to think of other things . . .'

HOME

The mansion house across the loch has been an important part of our life for almost sixty years now; my father and his father before him, and almost every able-bodied man in the area, were involved in building and extending it. Not only the big house, but the farm, the steadings, the gate lodges, workers' houses and jetty. It has the nicest view, across towards Ardnish and the islands from its own bay.

Everything was brought in by boat. The puffer came around the corner from Glenuig, belching black smoke and giving a hoot of its horn to get everyone down to help. It arrived at high tide and charged straight onto the shore to beach itself on its iron bottom. There was then a frantic few hours as a couple of horses and carts were taken onto the sand and all the chimneys, wooden planks or bags of cement were unloaded before the tide came in and the boat was floated off again to head back to Glasgow.

There must have been a dozen men working there at any one time, either on the house, building a jetty by the boat-house, or on the hill cutting peat. Father worked there for about ten years, helping to build a long wing onto the east side. He is very good with his hands and can fix just about anything. The old house has a four-storey tower and a square behind where the horses are kept, where my father stayed with Ewan Cameron. The owners of Roshven, the Blackburns, looked after all their workmen. In the middle of the day, a big bowl of soup or stew would be handed out.

The Blackburns loved having guests when they were younger and there was often a steamer or sailing boat in the bay. Father would put on his Clanranald piping uniform and go and play a few jigs for them while they were having their supper. He used to tell me about all the famous guests they had to stay, including Ruskin, Landseer and even Disraeli.

Mrs Blackburn was a very accomplished artist and she would paint pictures of the birds and plants, as well as family and guests. She became a good friend of my mother, although she was much older. They had both lived in Glasgow at some stage. They enjoyed talking about recent discoveries, or some bird they had not seen before in the area. Mrs Blackburn published a book called *Birds of Moidart*. She gave my mother a copy. Well thumbed now.

On Ardnish, about half a mile beyond the schoolhouse, is a beautiful crescent of sand about 300 yards long. It is pure white and it squeaks as you walk on it. It's made of very fine coral and known as 'the singing sands'. When they had people staying, the Blackburns and their guests would row across with lunch and have a picnic on the beach. Or they would go to Goat Island, which sits at the mouth of our loch and has an ancient fort at the top. There, they would pick brambles and play games with their young.

Now and again, we would all go across and play in a big shinty match at Roshven Farm. Everyone in the area would come together, a ceilidh would be held at night, and the day was always the event of the year.

I was just a youngster but I vaguely remember Queen Victoria's Jubilee in 1897. There were several beacons of fire at Roshven, and we lit three on Ardnish, and when ours were ablaze that triggered those above Arisaig and on the Rhu peninsula, too. I remember my father giving me a piggy-back up the hill and cooking sausages on the embers late at night. We could even see those on Eigg in the distance. There was a chain all around the coast of Britain and on every hill.

Anyway, back to the shinty. All the lairds were there: the Cameron-Heads from Lochailort, the Astley-Nicholsons from Arisaig, and the Stewarts from Kinlochmoidart. Each of them had a shinty team, and wagers were placed. There were other teams from all around as well, maybe ten teams of twenty men and children, even with some women playing, too.

Whisky would flow freely, and there would be old scores to settle, of course. The competition at one stage became a bit of a fight, but everything was soon patched up. One unexpected team comprised Irish navvies, who were building the railway extension from Fort William to Mallaig and had heard about the games from the Lochailort men at the Inn. They had had some practice with hurling and went into the tackles so hard there were bodies littering the field in minutes.

The final was between them and the Glenuig fishermen, and it was a full-time job stopping war from breaking out. It is said a bottle of whisky and a fight are sure to follow each other amongst the Irish, and thus it was that day.

The Irish won fair and square, and hands were shaken before the food was produced and the dancing got going. Old Professor Blackburn stood up and presented a keg of beer to the Irish for winning and a huge cheer went up.

A story went round from the Irish which everyone wanted to hear. The railway viaduct at Loch na Uamh was being built at the time. Starting at the Arisaig end, it stretched two hundred yards long and was twenty yards high. The shuttering was up, and horses and their carts of wet concrete were being backed towards the half-full pillar. At a certain point, they would be stopped, and a couple of men would shovel the concrete out and go and get some more.

There was one difficult horse, always kicking out when men passed, making contact as often as not and making life difficult for its carter. When it started backing towards the pillar, it just wouldn't stop and, despite desperate attempts from Paddy, the wee man from Kilkenny who had scored the winning goal at the shinty, the wagon went backwards into the wet concrete, followed by the horse.

Paddy danced a wee jig, we were told, and they just kept topping up the pillar until it was full of concrete. 'That bloody nag will be making the Almighty's life misery now,' said our storyteller.

After the shinty loss, one wag from Glenuig remarked that it was a pity Paddy hadn't gone into the concrete with the horse and cart.

WAR

I finish my story. 'Let's see what we can find you to eat,' I say to Louise.

'I couldn't eat a thing,' she replies. 'It'll just come straight up again.'

'A wee bit of bread, washed down with water,' I coax. 'You must have it, your body will need it.'

'More stories, DP,' Louise murmurs, closing her eyes.

I am frantic with worry. She's usually so cheerful, never stops talking to draw breath. Now, she just lies, curled up and silent.

I continue . . .

HOME

The other big get-together in the area was at haymaking time. The horses would go back and forth pulling the cutter and laying the grass in tidy rows, and a couple of days later, it would be turned over with long wooden rakes so that the other side could dry in the sun and the wind.

The last part involved every man, woman and child making stacks. A triangle of wooden poles would be erected in a spot where there was a good pile of hay, and, using a pitchfork, the hay would be pulled together into a sheaf and hoisted onto the stack until it was maybe eight feet high. It would be raked down to pull out the loose hay and tidied up, and then a canvas hood would be put over the top to shed the rain.

Haymaking time holds some of my best childhood memories. When the sun was out and everyone was involved, us children would run around playing and the adults seemed to tolerate us tunnelling under the hay or chasing each other around.

The old Blackburns would come down with their horse and trap laden with juice and scones, as everyone was taking a breather in the heat of the day. A week or two later, when the wind had had a chance to blow through the stacks to dry them and we had a good dry spell, a horse would be tied up to the big cart and the hay would be carted along to the square. We could sit on top of the rocking pile of hay, enjoying the sensation as it wobbled and we dodged under branches.

WAR

Louise smiles and squeezes my hand. I embellish the fun and the romantic life we led in these tales, because I don't want her to know of the bits that weren't so good.

For instance, I don't tell her that in the depths of winter it rains day after day so you think it will never stop. How, sometimes, every bit of clothing we had would be soaked through, and we would cough and sneeze all day long with cold, and mother would worry half to death that we'd catch pneumonia. How many children died when they were tiny, and how getting to a doctor or a hospital was well nigh impossible. From January until early summer, food was short, sometimes desperately so.

I know that Louise's life in the Valleys and the brutal poverty of life in a coal mining family is something she wants to forget. My life is the utopia she dreamed of.

Chapter 11

WAR

As Louise sleeps fitfully, I sit and fret. I hear movement in the undergrowth and freeze.

'It's only me.' Prissie drops down beside us. 'I've found a doctor. He's really old. I think we can trust him. Have you been giving her plenty of water?'

She fusses around Louise. 'Are you feeling any better, darling?' She helps Louise into a sitting position and pours more water from the gourd into her mouth. Louise drinks obediently. 'I'm to go to him very early tomorrow,' Prissie continues. 'He knows what Louise's symptoms are and he's trying to find some medicine.'

'How on earth did you find a doctor?' I ask.

'I just said the word "doctor" to the woman in the shop. She looked at me very intently, then she spoke to me and when I smiled and raised my hands, she knew I couldn't understand her. But she was friendly and she took me down the street and knocked on a door. It was as easy as that.'

Prissie settles back and continues her story. 'I feel quite comfortable wandering around by myself. There are so few people around, and those who are seem to be old women. There's hardly any cover, though. It's the flattest land you've ever seen. I'm not sure how we can get both of you into the port, but there's no rush. Let's see what the doctor says.'

I feel around the bag. 'No food left, Prissie. I'm so sorry.'

'I'll go and see what I can find tomorrow. It seems to be a farming area. There must be some food somewhere. Let's get a fire going, DP. We're well hidden here.'

I tell Prissie how wonderful she is, being the scout, the provider and the nurse. I'm almost in tears with relief.

It's a terrible night, though. Louise is getting weaker and Prissie is seriously worried. 'She's not keeping the water in her, and she's really dehydrated. I'm going to fill the gourd up in the village and then wait for the doctor. I want to be there early.'

Louise lies with her head on my chest and I caress her hair. 'You'll be all right,' I say, not quite believing my own words. 'A doctor is on the way'. We talk about her family for a spell, of the expectation of failure and a hard life, but speaking of her mother leaves her listless and depressed, and so I change the conversation.

'In our family it's the opposite,' I admit. 'We see opportunity, fun and goodness. It was my mother who brought this spirit to the family, and it's been good for the whole of Peanmeanach – not just for us.'

When Prissie returns with the doctor he seems surprised to see me. He was no doubt expecting only a sick woman, but he is polite to me. He has salt tablets for Louise.

'Perfect,' Prissie beams. 'These will allow you to keep the water in you.'

Prissie talks to the doctor in English, though he doesn't seem to understand a word. She acts out everything, like a game. Words like 'English', 'Gallipoli' and 'soldier' he grasps. He sees we have no food. And he seems to understand that we want to get to Alexandroupolis. Prissie is pleased when he uses the Greek pronunciation; she thinks it's a good sign.

The doctor gets up to go and shakes our hands firmly. He takes Prissie with him, to get food. My job is to get Louise to drink a bit of water, every hour at least, and to give her the salt tablets. By the evening, I think she is getting a little stronger. She wants to sit up rather than lie on the ground.

Prissie returns with an armful of wonderful-smelling fresh bread, some honey and eggs. She also has a knife and a small pan to boil water and make coffee.

I cross myself and thank God.

Louise manages to eat a scrap of bread, and Prissie is overjoyed. 'Oh sweetheart, I was beginning to get seriously worried about you. Another couple of days in that condition and we might have lost you.'

The next morning, the doctor appears again, accompanied by a friendly little plump woman. They have brought us blankets and some more bread. The woman wants us to come with her to a place where we can shelter; they think there's going to be heavy rain.

We gather our kit together and follow the woman to a well-hidden bothy by the marsh, possibly a fishing hut. Prissie and the woman help Louise there. Much better, we all agree, than camping out in the open air. The woman points at herself and says, 'Eleni'. We introduce ourselves, too, and there are lots of smiles. We feel a bit more relaxed now. We trust this couple.

Prissie looks around and grins. 'My dad had a shed to get away from Mum, too,' she says.

'My friend Sandy would have loved this place,' I say. 'We would have enough fish by now to feed us for the next week.' I remember how much I enjoyed fishing with him and my father. Peaceful times. I wonder if I'll ever fish again.

If my shoulder was better I could guddle a fish or two. I'd seen Sandy do it many times; he would lie on his front on the bank with one hand in the water. The fish would come up to see what was going on and he would gently caress its belly with his finger. It would become a bit lethargic, and then with a flick he would have it on the bank. I'll bet that would impress Louise.

*

The doctor insists that we rest here until Louise's strength returns. And so the days pass: cold and wet some days, sunny on others, plenty of wood for a fire, and Eleni coming down with food every day.

We itch to be off. The attractions of the little bothy have long worn off, and it feels more like a prison. Sensing our frustration one evening, the doctor says in clear English, 'Tomorrow.'

True to his word, he returns the following morning. This time, he is accompanied by a different woman. She speaks fluent English, which is wonderful.

'You're British!' I exclaim excitedly.

'No, I'm Greek,' she replies, 'but I have lived in London. Please call me Maria. It's not my real name, but we need to protect the doctor. I'm here to help you get back to safety, but I won't tell him what's going to happen.'

With a cup of coffee in one hand and a cigarette in the other, she tells us her plan. 'On Saturdays, there is a market in Dedeagach . . .'

' Alexandroupolis,' interjects the helpful doctor.

'There will be donkeys and carts coming from all over the country with things to sell. I'll come here to fetch you, and we'll be met on the outskirts of Ferres on Friday night. You'll go separately into the port, and at the market I'll meet you again. You'll then be reunited at a safe house and await further instructions. You are lucky to have met the doctor here. He is Greek, a good man. Now, I must go. See you on Friday.'

We love speculating about her. 'She must be here to spy on the Bulgars, to report back to Britain,' Louise suggests. 'Do you think there are lots of people like her? What a dangerous job! How boring we are being nurses, Prissie, when we could be like her!'

Louise and Prissie are clearly in awe of Maria; as am I, if the truth be told.

That night, I ask Prissie if she has ever really loved a man.

She shifts uncomfortably, and I immediately regret asking.

'No, not really,' she tells me. 'There was a boy I fancied like mad at school, but he didn't even look at me, and then it was straight into nursing training. I love being with you two, though, proper little lovebirds. You couldn't get a cigarette paper between you both since you arrived at the clearing station.'

'Well,' Louise pipes up, 'DP is the first and last for me. I'm keeping him.'

I sit with a happy smile on my face and lean across to take Louise's hand. 'I'm lucky to be alive and I'm lucky to have you,' I reply. 'Both of you, in fact.'

*

Come Friday morning, we clear up and prepare for departure, not wanting anyone to know the place has been occupied.

Maria turns up on schedule and tells us the rules. 'Don't talk at all, and never look me. Don't look at each other, either. If the army catches you, you'll have to go it alone, I'm afraid. We can't jeopardise the plan.'

I flush. What a thought! After all we have come through, would I be able to keep quiet if I saw Louise arrested in front of me? I decide to make sure I am arrested, too. But I nod obediently without catching Louise's eye.

'When we get to the market I'll come past you. If I have a bag on my shoulder, then you can follow me. If not, I'll come around again. If the coast is clear and the bag's on my shoulder, follow me. It all depends on whether or not we are being watched. DP, I'll collect Louise first. She will take you by the hand and lead you in case you stumble. Are you all right with that?'

I sense this is a joke at my expense, so laughingly I agree.

'We need to get the bandage off your eye. It will attract too much attention and people will remember it. I've brought you some glasses. We have about an hour to walk, but it's easy going.'

Maria and Prissie go on ahead to make sure we don't bump into anyone, and Louise and I follow, hand in hand. It is raining hard and my glasses steam up. I can barely see a thing, but Louise guides me.

'The rain is good,' says Maria. 'It will keep the army off the road. Less conspicuous, too, walking in pairs than four of us walking together.'

We arrive safely at the outskirts of Ferres and take shelter under a tree. I am the first to go. An old man and woman with a mule and a cart full of baskets stop beside the road.

Louise embraces me and tearfully wishes me luck.

No introductions are made, and only Maria speaks. 'You'll be uncomfortable, DP, I'm afraid. You have about ten hours in there.'

I crawl into a pile of blankets on the cart and arrange myself comfortably, with my bag as a pillow. The baskets are rearranged around me, and off we go. Within a short time, I am in severe pain; every stone we jolt over causes me to wince. I am glad I am lying on my good shoulder, but I can't turn over.

As we trundle along the track, I can hear murmuring from the couple up front and an occasional greeting from passers by. I am so stiff and sore I decide to think of something else, something good. I shut my eyes and imagine a year from now, heading home with Louise.

*

We'll get off the train at Lochailort. My parents won't know we're coming. It'll be spring, with flowers and young birds and animals everywhere. We'll walk hand in hand down the path, and I'll point out the lochs where Angus and I fished and swam, an eagle gliding on the skyline. I'll tell Louise again the stories that she already knows by heart. We'll sit at the highest point of the peninsula and I'll point out Inverailort Castle, Roshven and Arisaig House. We will slowly meander down towards the village, wanting to take as long as we can, and yet at the same time dying to hurry. I'll be desperate to show off Louise to my parents and everyone in Peanmeanach.

The dogs will see us first and bark, bringing people to the back door to see what has interested them. 'A man, it looks like DP! But who's the girl?' The excitement, the tears. Yes, we're engaged.

*

I smile to myself. Louise would love the place, and adore the people, and I know they would love her, too. It feels so remote from this cart, this landscape, this situation; I feel a tear trickle down my face.

I lapse into semi-consciousness, which is a blessing for a while. But after a time, I am woken with a start. The cart has pulled up, and I can hear raised voices. Men are questioning the old couple. I lie there, afraid to breathe, sweating despite the chill and terrified of feeling the baskets being pulled off me.

But luckily the men don't search us. Maybe the task is too arduous at this early hour, or the elderly couple too innocent-looking. And so the cart slowly begins to rattle along again.

We arrive at the marketplace before dawn. I can hear the sounds of people setting up their stalls and laying out their produce for the day. I emerge stiffly out of my hellhole to find myself in an alleyway. I am directed to a wall in the square by the old man who has brought me here. My blood begins to flow and my aches and pains subside a little. There is so much bustle and noise as the town centre fills up with traders and customers. Soon a hot cup of coffee is thrust into my hand and I begin to feel more human again.

I can smell the sea, the cheeses and meats. I wonder where Louise and Prissie are, and how they are faring.

The winter sun is pleasant on my face as I sit enjoying the busy activity. And then I feel her beside me. What a relief! I desperately want to embrace her. Louise takes my hand, squeezes it and leads me off, with not even a chance to thank the couple who have ferried me here. Within minutes we are up some stairs and in someone's home. Maria is there and so is Prissie.

'It's so good to see you both,' I say. 'We were stopped, but luckily they didn't search the cart. I was shaking like a leaf.'

'Is everyone all right?' Maria asks.

'Exhausted,' says Prissie. 'I had to carry a load of vegetables on my back all the way here, while you were lying in luxury in your carriage, DP!'

'You can share your stories later,' says Maria. 'I need to tell you what's happening next. This property is owned by a successful engineer who has gone missing. He was against the Bulgars and made it obvious, so they took him and his wife off. They've ransacked the place once, and we don't think they'll be back. No one can see into it, and it's got a lock, so you should be safe. But no lights or fires please. Girls, you can go out, but not together and maybe only once a day. Act with a sense of purpose, as if you're going somewhere. DP, not you I'm afraid. There are no young men in this town. They've all been conscripted, so you would be too obvious. I'll get you some food and come back before midday.'

At lunch we eat the best food in months: salami, cheeses, dates and raisins washed down with ouzo. Everyone smokes. We sit at a proper table, and use a knife and fork. It is such a pleasure.

Maria won't tell us her plan. 'You'll know when the time comes. You'll have to stay here for several days while I get everything organised. There are packs of cards and a chess-board to keep you entertained for a while. We're also expecting another guest – a pilot who was shot down. I don't know when he'll come. Please leave a bed for him.'

'Could we have a bath, Maria?' Louise asks. 'We've been travelling for two months now and we need to wash our clothes. We're filthy, and my hair is horrid.'

'Tonight,' says Maria. 'Stay up very late, say around one in the morning, then light a fire. Let's hope no one sees the smoke. You can have a night of cleaning and scrubbing, no need to get up in the morning. No candles, though. You'll have to do everything in the kitchen by firelight. And remember to hang your clothes inside the house to dry, not outside.'

Louise and I are sharing a big bed. 'Let's not get into it until we're clean,' she whispers. 'It's a special moment for us.'

We lie slumped in the living area until we are woken by Prissie. 'Your turn, lovebirds,' she trills as she heads off to her room, giggling. Filling the tub with water heated by the blazing fire, what excitement it is for me to give Louise a bath. The room smells of scented lavender soap, and we have a proper towel – what a luxury. While we had moments of intimacy during the trip, it tended to be an embrace on the cold hard ground or in an attic with Prissie sleeping alongside us.

The night passes quickly with our lovemaking, alternating between passion and tenderness. Louise is so sweet and gentle, my heart bursts with love for her.

*

Prissie is excited about the pilot arriving, but it is another three days before he does.

In the middle of the night we are woken by soft, insistent taps on the front door. Louise tiptoes to open it, terrified it will be the Bulgars, but the English voice on the other side whispers, 'Let me in.'

The pilot is there by himself, his guide having vanished before the door was opened. He is tall and good-looking. His name is Charlie. Prissie fell for him immediately, she later confesses. We sit around him as he drinks coffee and tells us what happened to him.

He was in a Sopwith Pup doing recce flights above Gallipoli and was shot at and hit. The plane lost power, its engine intermittent. He managed to fly it for a few miles north and away from the Turkish lines, but it became clear that he was going to have to crash-land into trees. He managed to parachute out, but his gunner didn't make it. He saw the plane hit the ground and burst into flames.

We quiz him about the evacuation. He tells us the allied forces got out before Christmas. Everyone. No casualties. 'Typical,' he says. 'The only thing our generals have done well in this war is organise a retreat. The troops from Gallipoli are moving back to Egypt and the Western Front. There will be a big push on in Thessaloniki, too, I believe.'

'The Lovat Scouts will be there then,' I volunteer.

He has been trying to find out where the Turkish army is heading – back to Constantinople, or here to Bulgaria and then Thessaloniki.

Charlie was rescued by a Sarakatsani farming family, who hid him for a week. Then, like us, partisans retrieved him and here he is. He is terribly posh and terribly charming, and Prissie flirts outrageously with him. He says 'splendid' and 'jolly' and words we would never use, and she keeps telling him how brave he is and shouting, 'Oh, well done you.'

Louise just shakes her head and tells me that it's all a bit unseemly, but I can't agree with her. 'It's the war, Louise,' I say, 'people seize the moment.'

Chapter 12

With the candles flickering in the corner and a bottle of ouzo on the table, Charlie laments the fact that there is no whisky.

'We need a good malt, DP,' he complains, 'not this filthy stuff.' He raises his glass and contemplates the clear liquid.

Louise pipes up. 'DP knows how to make whisky. He lived with his uncle on an island distilling it and keeping clear of the police. Tell us about it.'

'It might take a while,' I say . . .

HOME

I had finished school and wanted to get away from the village for a spell. We talked about Glasgow and Inverness, maybe going to see Sheena in Canada, although there was no money for the fare.

'Tearlach on the isle of Canna needs a hand,' my father suggested. 'He's getting old. Cutting the peat and carrying the bags of barley about is difficult for him. And there's so much demand for his whisky he can't make it fast enough.

You would have a good time too, I think. It's a great island, not quiet like home.'

It was settled. After the hay was made in July, I would be off.

There was a load of hay being shipped to Tarbert in Loch Nevis from Canna, and I could get a lift on the returning boat. I'd been told to be there by the end of the month. And so, with a pack on my back, I headed off to Morar, where I stayed with some friends on the first day, and then continued along the lochside and over the hill to Donald Macdonald, a kinsman of ours in Tarbert.

A few days later, a small steam launch stacked high with good dry hay and towing a big rowing boat came around the corner and into the bay. At high tide she was pulled up as far as she would go, and a long day was spent loading the hay onto a cart and unloading it again into the byre. The next day we were off, with me in the rowing boat along with Iain Mackinnon and two heifers. They just stood chewing the cud as the boat rocked from side to side. I would never have believed this could happen.

'It's how it's always done on the islands,' said Iain. 'They never jump overboard.'

We stopped at Mallaig overnight so Iain could pick up supplies. Box after box was loaded on, with a couple of scythes, a wheelbarrow, some brandy for the laird and several bags of seed. The steam launch was well laden as we set off for the ten-mile trip to Canna.

Tearlach was at the jetty when we arrived, talking in English to Mr Thom, the laird.

'Here you are, young Donald! Let's be off. We'll spend the night with a lady friend of mine, get my messages in the shop first thing and go to the Nunnery tomorrow.'

He was a big, strong man, with greying red hair and a thick beard. He must have been seventy years old, but I had to step out to keep up with him. As we walked he pointed things out to me. Canna was a lovely island, very fertile, with lots of people living on it. Tearlach said there must be half a dozen my age – including the Mackinnon girls.

'Look, Donald Peter, that's our new Catholic church – St Edward's – built by the Marquess of Bute for us. He's the richest man in Britain, they say. And over there are two carved crosses over a thousand years old.'

I was impressed.

'And look at these cattle, fantastic bulls. The best Highland cattle in the world are on this wee island.'

It was clear he was very proud of his home.

'Why is your home called the Nunnery, Uncle Tearlach?'

'Well, at the same time as Saint Columba got to Iona some nuns came to Canna and decided this was the place to build their convent.'

This all seemed fairly logical until I saw what a difficult place they had chosen for their home.

We got there about midday. 'Here we are,' Tearlach announced as we reached the top of a rise.

There was nothing. No wall or building, and a cliff plummeting down to the sea on the left. He guided me to a rope to hang on to, and we climbed down 200 feet to the shore. There, right against the rocks, was a house, and a couple of outbuildings which must have been the distillery.

'Home sweet home, DP. You'll be a grand help to me. I haven't made a drop of *uisge beatha* in six months,' he said regretfullly.

'Why not?'

'We're waiting for the bere from Tiree and a few bags of malt, too. It will come as soon as their harvest is finished, in a month or so. But there's lots to be done before then.'

I carried pail after pail of water from the place where it tumbled down the cliff, to be heated up, and then with the pony 'up top' fetched a good ton of peat to where we could lower it in buckets down the cliff. We scrubbed the floor of the barn that was used to ferment the barley, cleaned the tuns and the copper still, and scrubbed the five-gallon milk pails that were used to transport the whisky. Then the boat was sanded and repainted, and finally all was set for the start of the distilling.

Tearlach was a keen teacher. 'The first thing you need to know, lad, is that the less people know what we're doing the better. Now islanders, they know, and we swap our whisky for their peat, food, help with transport and such like. The laird never mentions it, but he knows fine and benefits from our good work. He's a good sort. Outwith the island, you need to keep it in the family! We have Hector, my cousin from Tiree, who brings in the bere and the malt, and Angus John in Kinlochmoidart and Ruaridh in Arisaig who sell it. Nobody else knows. If you're asked, I'm crofting – and poorly – and you're helping out.'

We sat by the fire with the wind whistling down the chimney and the waves crashing on the rocks only feet away from us.

He was in a talkative mood. 'It's a great time to be making whisky,' he said, 'as long as you don't get caught. The prime minister just last year raised tax to fifteen shillings a gallon, so the big distillers are really suffering, and if wasn't for us, ordinary people couldn't afford their drams. We can get a grand price and we're still a fraction of the money your father's friend, Colonel Macdonald, sells his Long John for.'

With a smile he raised his glass. 'To Lloyd George, *slainte*.'

He told me about the excise men. 'They're the gaugers and entitled to fifty per cent of the proceeds of what they seize. They have a dangerous man in Fort William, an outsider from Aberdeen called Andrew Leslie, and we're in his area. He has spies who tip him off. I used to do a run into Mallaig, but there were a few close shaves and I'm certain Leslie was getting news. Even ten years ago there were three stills along Loch Shiel, but he raided them and smashed up the stills. Simon Fraser was caught and spent a year in jail. There was a convoy of six ponies with panniers of twenty-pint jars of whisky on its way to Glasgow, heading over the drove road above Spean Bridge in the dark one winter's night, and he lay in wait with some soldiers and seized it. John Cameron was lucky and he managed to run off into the hill when he heard them coming.'

Tearlach always enjoyed a story about daring exploits where the smugglers or illegal distillers had been tipped off about a raid, and a fool was made of the gauger.

Just after dawn one early autumn morning there was a bang on the door.

'Are you there, ye big hairy monster? It's the hard-working Protestants delivering while you soft Catholics are still in your beds.'

I was introduced, then watched as three men wolfed down bowls of porridge and tea while Hector and Tearlach caught up on the news. Then Hector and his three men unloaded the sacks of barley from the boat and headed off.

'Not a moment to waste, DP,' Tearlach explained. 'We need to make a start straight away and get the whisky to the mainland before the winter storms start.'

So, the first batch of barley, or bere as he called it, was mixed with water and put into a vast forty-gallon pot with a gentle fire below it, to 'steep' for three days and nights. Softened, it was then left to cool for a day and spread onto a floor for nine days to germinate. It was then shovelled into the kiln, where a good heat was given to it – hot work for me, as I had to turn it every hour until it was dry and keep the peat fire topped up too.

Tearlach had a stone wheel and a bowl with a hole in it, and I would shovel the dried bere into it and he would turn the wheel, milling the grain into a flour. We then wheeled the bere across to a wee building right beside the waterfall where it was put into a vat and boiling water added to make a mash. I stirred it very carefully while Tearlach added just the right amount of malt for taste. We would let it bubble and boil, but gently so as not to spoil it.

That done, the liquid would be drained off into a tank, leaving the draff which Iain Mackinnon was desperate to get his hands on to feed his beloved bulls. The liquid was then put into Tearlach's pride and joy – his copper still.

'It was used by my great-grandfather in South Uist,' he said, patting it, 'and it was made in Glasgow.'

A good fire would be going, and the vapour would go up the spout and down into a copper coil, where cold water would be run over it continuously to condense it, and with that, the first still of very rough *uisge beatha* was complete.

'By God, Donald Peter, don't you go drinking it! Your hair would fall out. You could strip the paint off the door with that stuff. Men die being too keen to get at the dram.'

So we poured it back into the copper still twice more until it was just the thing.

We did this again and again until we had five batches made and every barrel, milk pail and jar was full. It was funny how many visitors would 'just happen to be passing' from around the island, often carrying a stone jar – 'by coincidence'.

'Now,' Tearlach explained, 'the right thing to do is to sit and let it mature in wooden barrels for three years, but that's not our job. We need to get it across to cousins Angus John and Ruaridh and get some money for it. Hector will be across with our second lot of bere for the winter's work, and we need to have money to pay him and get our containers back.'

Meanwhile, there would be a bit of socialising. Tearlach was a very popular guest, always with a wee bottle in his pocket for his host. There was a reel in the barn one night when the men returned with money in their pockets from the cattle sales on the mainland, and we were always visiting the people of the island, enjoying the *craic* and waiting for a calm spell when we could make our deliveries.

I was sent to get Sean and Archie, two young men my age, and together we loaded up the boat and set off for Arisaig one cold winter's day, well before daylight. It was a ten-mile row, and the boat was laden down, so we took it in turns.

Tearlach was nervous. He knew that this was when the gaugers would be most likely to catch him. But we arrived safely at Rhu farm, where Ruaridh, with the help of Tearlach, tasted and approved the quality, and a large amount of money changed hands. My cousin was a happy man. We ate well and collapsed exhausted after the hard trip across. The next day we emptied all the containers into casks that he had stored in a wee cave in the hill above the house. Here, he had dozens and dozens of stone jars from the big legal distillers – Long John, Ben Nevis, Dewars, White Horse and many more. He would decant the whisky into these and the excise man would know no better when he saw the jars.

Sandy was working at the hotel in Arisaig for the winter, so I took the other two lads and, armed with a bottle of our homemade Long John, we walked down to spend the evening with him. The talk that night was all about setting up our own wee distillery on Ardnish.

Sandy was determined to get the business going. 'What we need, DP, is a good water supply, a handy bank of peat, an inlet in the rocks where we can get a boat in easily and unload it, plus a few good buildings with rock behind so the smoke can't be seen. The west end of the point it has to be, otherwise the gaugers would see everything with a telescope from Roshven.' It seemed he had worked everything out. 'The Bochan lives at Port an t-Sluichd – that's just the place. There must be half a dozen derelict houses there!' he added excitedly.

My goodness, we were in some state as we hiccuped and staggered our way back after breakfast the next morning, not having had a wink of sleep following a steady night of downing the drams.

Sandy was keen to come back to the Nunnery with me. 'I need to learn,' he said. 'Whisky is the best chance we have to make a living in Peanmeanach.'

I told him to stay there and figure out how we would sell it. We knew that's where the money was.

WAR

'You must do it, DP,' Prissie exclaims. 'One day you could make it legal, and it would be the distillery everyone talked about.'

'I'd name it "Sandy's Whisky",' I say, 'in his memory.' I raise my glass of ouzo in a salute to him with a tear in my eye. '*Slainte*, Sandy.'

*

Louise and I had been the new loves, but we now feel like an old married couple with Prissie and Charlie's raw passion. It is strange.

In the evenings, Louise and Prissie go for a walk, down to the fishing port and along the shore. They see the occasional soldier but no one else other than children or the elderly.

We still have no idea what the plan is, although we are fairly sure that we will be heading off on a fishing boat. We don't even know the destination. Possibly up the coast, to neutral Greece?

'Athens is meant to be beautiful,' volunteers Charlie. 'Lovely architecture, the centre of the world in days gone by. I'm sure we could manage a couple of weeks there for a holiday before we try to get back to Blighty.'

We all agree that this would be perfect, though in truth I long more than anything in the world to return to Ardnish, as soon as humanly possible.

Maria comes by late one night and tells us to pack up and be ready first thing. We have to prepare some food and leave the place immaculate. Our transport is ready. There is great excitement. Better times seem to lie ahead. Different times, anyway.

At dawn, she returns. 'Let's go. Prissie, you and Charlie come first, and I'll see you onto the boat. Fifteen minutes from now, Louise and DP, meet me at the port entrance.'

We'd been in the safe cocoon of the house for so long – now we would be running the gauntlet. We embrace each other tightly before we depart.

Louise and I hurry through Alexandroupolis to the port. Without a word, we are helped over the side and lowered down into the hold of a fishing boat. It stinks of fish, and we have only crates to sit on.

'The two brothers who own the boat speak no English,' Maria informs us. 'They will take you to Lemnos, where the Gallipoli fleet is based. It is a two-day trip. The first couple of hours will be the most dangerous, so stay down here until the skipper comes to get you. When you're out of sight of land you'll be quite safe. When you get to Lemnos, report immediately to the hospital. They'll look after things from there. The *Gloucester Castle* will be there, girls.'

We kiss Maria and gush with gratitude, telling her how kind she is, how wonderful. I invite her to visit me in Ardnish and she laughs.

We are sorry not to see the town from the sea as we head off, with only the reek of diesel and fish to think about. The journey is dreadful: smelly, dirty, cold, and the brothers unfriendly. They have no interest in helping us or making us comfortable. Charlie asks them if he could boil some water for coffee and they reluctantly agree.

During the day, we sit up top, but come night we shelter from the wind and cold below deck.

'I wonder why they are doing this trip?' Louise asks me in a low voice.

'Maybe they have family on Lemnos, or perhaps they're going to load up with guns for the partisans.'

But in truth we have no idea.

Louise becomes violently sick as the boat rises and falls in the swell, and eats next to nothing the whole way across. Prissie remains as chirpy as ever, and Charlie keeps us amused with jokes and stories, though they all seem to concern crashing planes and dead comrades.

All of his fellow pilots seem to have ridiculous names – such as Bunter Benjie, so named because he was fat, or

Tash, on account of the chap's splendid moustache – and to live in stately homes. Several seem to be Lord something or other. Prissie teases him mercilessly and calls him 'Champagne Charlie', soon abbreviated to 'Champagne'.

'Can you see any ships, Champagne?' she asks, eyes full of mischief.

He adores her.

*

We arrive at last in Lemnos. All of us, apart from Charlie, had passed through here on the way to Gallipoli; Prissie and Louise had been three times. The bay has fewer ships; we count only eleven and not a single hospital ship among them.

As we get off the fishing boat there is barely a grunt from our hosts despite our cheery farewells. 'Damn rude,' declares Charlie.

'Let's have a few moments to ourselves,' I suggest. 'The military will control our destiny the minute we walk into the hospital, and I'm not sure I'm ready.'

So we sit on a wall in the harbour. Prissie bursts into tears. She knows that Charlie will be whisked off to an officers' mess immediately. She's inconsolable; they'd only had a week together. He promises to stay in touch with her and assures her that this isn't the end of their friendship. Louise and I are doubtful; privately, we are convinced he's married, perhaps with children.

*

We soon discover we are quite the heroes. No one has come across anybody who has escaped overland from Gallipoli.

We are invited to meet the base commandant, an elderly naval officer, and his staff, who all want to hear our story. There are about a dozen senior ranks there, which is quite intimidating. We tell them about the Christians who were our saviours, the massacre of the Armenian Christians by the Turks, the support in the south of Bulgaria for the allies, and the splendid job done by the enigmatic Maria. They are fascinated by our account and take lots of notes.

'We'll send you back to Malta in a few days, Gillies, but in the meantime, you need to see a doctor. Girls, you need to report to the Queen Alexandra matron at the hospital. Charlie, there's a ship going to Gibraltar tonight. You should take that. They're desperately short of pilots and will be glad to see you.'

It is so much quieter than when I was last here. Most of the injured are back in Malta or Egypt at the big hospitals there. We are told that almost everyone will be off Lemnos within a month. Louise and Prissie are put in a tent on their own, and I am billeted with some young naval conscripts who have been nowhere near the war yet. They treat me as if I am of their fathers' generation, although I am not yet twenty-two.

Prissie is despondent as Charlie climbs aboard the tender that will take him out to his ship. She talks about how precious those few days were, how she'll never forget him.

Louise and I know there is little chance of him seeing the war out; Prissie does too, I suspect. We don't talk about it, of course. He will be sent to France, where every gun will be trained on his plane as he flies over the trenches with a cameraman hanging over the side to photograph the German lines.

*

For a few days, it is, indeed, like a holiday. The leaves are coming out on the trees and everyone walks around with a smile on their faces. It is hard to comprehend that a battle has been lost and tens of thousands slaughtered so close to here, as we relax on the beach in the warmth, drinking lemonade and dining on delicious fish. Prissie joins us when she's not in the naval ward room – pretty girls are always welcome there. I receive a full medical check-up from one of the ship's medics. The shoulder is stronger now, but I need lots of exercise to build up the muscle again. I'm still skin and bones, of course, but with Louise's care I'll soon put on weight.

He tells me that my bad eye is permanently damaged. 'It's a patch for life, Gillies, I'm sorry to say. But you're a very lucky man – the right eye is looking pretty good and you may well regain reasonable vision. Avoid too much bright light for now and rest your eyes frequently.'

*

The harbour at Malta is exhilarating. Our senses are bombarded with the hustle and bustle of the port, people rushing to and fro, and above all the constant backdrop of English voices. We have been away from civilisation for such a long time.

We talk often about what we're most looking forward to when we reach home. For me, it's a big breakfast of eggs, bacon and sausages. Prissie can't wait to go dancing again, while Louise wants a comfortable bed in which she'll stay for a whole day and night.

We report to the army HQ and log in our details. I am immediately sent to the Cottonera Hospital in Valletta for two days, where the doctors, including an eye surgeon, look over me. Louise tells me he is the best one, because that was where the Royal Army Medical Corps was based. All he does is confirm what the ship's medic had said in Lemnos, but it is a relief in a way.

I am wildly impatient to find out when I might be shipped home, but manage to keep it to myself. I know they won't hold onto wounded soldiers any longer than necessary, and that I am far from being the only one yearning for home.

Meanwhile, Louise and Prissie report to the Queen Alexandra Corps. Louise later tells me that they were met by a junior nurse who took their details and then consulted with an officer. To everyone's surprise, the most senior Queen Alexandra officer came to introduce herself.

'Staff Nurses Jones and O'Hara, I'm Colonel Thomas. I've just heard about your escape from Gallipoli. My congratulations. You will be talked about throughout the whole service. Not only that, but I gather it was you two who took the initiative and led the nurses onto Suvla beach to help out when the medical services were so stretched.'

She then invited the girls through to the staff room, where they were introduced to various nurses and doctors and made polite conversation as best they could.

Colonel Thomas clapped her hands. 'Ladies and gentlemen, we have two remarkable nurses here. Nurse O'Hara, why don't you tell us all about the mission to the beach in Gallipoli and then the trek back to Malta with your patient?'

Louise says that Prissie was in her element. With much gesturing and colourful language, she described our escape so vividly that even Louise was impressed by our bravery and daring.

When Prissie finished, there was much applause and shouts of 'bravo!' Colonel Thomas announced, 'The senior doctor on board the *Gloucester Castle* has written a citation, which I shall now read to you.' She took a letter from her coat pocket and began. ' "Nurses Jones and O'Hara were stationed on the hospital ship *Gloucester Castle* and were going about their duties. However, they could see that the ship was not coping with the volume of casualties. They arranged a team of fellow Queen Alexandra Corps nurse volunteers and went onto the beach, where they made a huge difference, evoking comparisons among the soldiers there of Florence Nightingale. I strongly recommend that their bravery and initiative be recognised with an award. Yours sincerely, Brigadier Doctor Pease." I am delighted to award you the Royal Red Cross Medal.'

Louise and Prissie had blushed with pleasure as Colonel Thomas pulled two medals from her pocket and pinned them onto their uniforms to much whooping and clapping.

*

'Your family will be so proud,' I say, as I look at the medal in my hand.

'I know. I just wish Dad was still alive. He'd be bragging down the pub like he'd won it himself.'

With time to kill while we await news of what is to happen to us, we find a room in the town and spend the days together. Louise becomes tanned, but I have to be careful; with my red hair and fair skin I burn easily, even in the weak spring sunshine.

The island is full of injured soldiers back from Gallipoli, with hospitals at every corner, it seems. Louise tells me she can see the hospital ships in the Grand Harbour from our room.

Louise takes my weight as her personal responsibility and devises a diet that involves a lot of green vegetables and eggs. She manages to get her hands on some cuts of meat most days, too. To my joy, she manages to persuade the hospital that what I most need is rest and good food, and that my bed in the hospital would be better used for other more seriously injured patients.

After their few days' leave, Louise and Prissie are set to work. Louise is sent to a hospital for the severely injured. She tells me of patients with third-degree burns all over their body and missing limbs. Prissie works in the officers' hospital, the Dragunara, where there are forty patients. It is run by the Red Cross, which is chronically understaffed.

Prissie loves seeing the big ships in the harbour. 'There's the *Braemar Castle*! And the *Dunluce*!' she exclaims. They had been passenger ships before the war, journeying to New York, Australia and places like that, and Prissie recognises them from their glory days, when they set sail from Liverpool on expensive long-distance cruises.

*

After two weeks, I receive a big bag of post. Louise tactfully leaves me alone with a cup of coffee, and I read my mail again and again. There are several letters from Mother, who thinks I am still in Gallipoli, asking what my trench is like and if I am getting fed properly. The last one is full of concern that she hasn't heard from me for two months, I've always been so good about keeping in touch.

The winter on the west coast has been a bad one, very cold with some snow. The milk cow has two calves and they are doing well. Christmas was a subdued affair, with no young people around, but everyone in Peanmeanach enjoyed a meal together and the Whaler and Aggie had some family over from Glenuig, so that was nice. She finishes up by writing: 'We need to hear from you, DP, are you still all right? We pray for you and Angus every day.'

Sheena has written a long letter from Canada. She's enjoying her work but wishes there were more young folk around. Winters are cold and the days short. She has read and re-read her books, and there are no more around. She's been learning to play the fiddle, as she's found to her delight that there's a great tradition of fiddle playing there. 'Every Monday night I walk an hour to Glencoe Mills and meet many others and we play together. We are practising for a ceilidh at New Year.' She hopes I am well and that Gallipoli wasn't as bad as was being reported in the papers.

There are two letters from Father Angus which I save for later. Suddenly, it is all too much. Although I wrote to my parents as soon as we arrived, I doubt whether they have received my letter, and it pains me to think of their suffering with worry. Peanmeanach may still be a long way away, but in my mind I can see my home as clear as day. I can smell the seaweed and the cattle, taste the fresh herring fried in oatmeal with tatties from the field.

I may be in a kind of paradise here in Malta with Louise, but my heart aches for home.

*

One night, we meet up with Prissie in a bar on the hill. Prissie puts her arm around Louise's shoulder. 'Are you well, darling? Feeling good?'

I remember this intimacy later. The bar is full of naval officers. Prissie loves being around officers, she always has. She tells us about the hospital where she is working. 'It's beautiful. It's in a villa owned by the Marchesa Scicluna – she gives the Red Cross the money to run it, too. The Marchesa lives in a cottage in the garden and comes up to talk to the officers every day. She's lovely.'

Prissie is determined to find out where Charlie has been posted, but so far has had no luck. She has written to him in Gibraltar.

Louise advises her tactfully to forget him. 'It was fun, Prissie, but you need to look forward now.'

Louise and I are like a married couple, living together in our one room; her coming home from work and me cooking dinner. My mother always had me helping to cook at home, so I have an idea of what to do. I buy a chicken and pluck it, add tomatoes, herbs, onions and peppers like the locals do, and we eat like royalty.

'Food will seem so bland when we get home,' I say to Louise, and apparently I repeat this every day.

All sorts of things happen in war that would not happen back home. If my father knew that I was sleeping with a girl without being married to her there would be a hell of a row. Louise thinks her mother would be much more understanding, but if her father were alive he would beat her to within an inch of her life. He was a real hypocrite, though, she says; she was sure he had another woman in a town nearby.

And so the days pass with me sleeping, eating and trying to improve my strength and fitness as well as gain weight. There are a lot of injured soldiers doing various sorts of rehabilitation when allowed leave from the hospitals. Many of us meet up at the port and sit on a wall, talk and play cards.

The Anzacs among us have a lot of money. They are paid six times as much as we are, but we all have enough, as we've been given our back pay from when we were at the front. With plentiful wine, good company and a warm sun, things are pretty good. I think of my parents, who have never come across wine. It's whisky or nothing at home. What would they think of their boy if they could see him now, sitting on the wall in shorts, a pretty girl on his arm, and a glass in his hand? I smile at the thought and the ache in my heart subsides a little.

I love so many things about being in Malta with Louise, but my anxiety to get home is growing. My parents need me to help sow the grass and make the hay. There are so few ships heading back to Britain. I am on a list, and if a vacancy becomes available I will hear, but the wait is now agonising.

Chapter 13

One Sunday morning, with the bells of the church ringing throughout the town, Louise tells me she has a picnic planned. She's bought cheese and chicken, and she's packed a gourd of wine and taken a blanket from the bed. After Mass, we walk to the main road out of town and hitch a lift from an army truck. We settle down on a beach and relax in the sunshine. Louise pours me some wine and lights a cigarette.

Unpacking the basket, and holding my gaze, she pulls out a tiny pair of canvas shoes and lays them in my hand.

It takes me a few seconds before I understand. 'Really? *Really?*'

She takes my hand and presses it to her stomach. 'Your baby is in there,' she says, looking into my eyes, willing me to be pleased. Which I am.

I raise my hand to her cheek, and she holds it there. I hold her close while tears of relief and joy stream down her face.

Louise thinks it must have happened on the night Prissie went into town in Turkey and met the priest. The first time we'd made love, to anyone, ever – and along comes a baby!

She had been feeling nauseous for some time but assumed that it must be the aftermath of the dysentery or the awful sea crossing. I confess that every time we have made love I've been sure she would get pregnant – and is that not what has now happened?

We lie in the sand all afternoon, talking about how our lives will change and what our families will think. The first grandchild in either family. I know my mother will be delighted.

I ask Louise to marry me and come back to Ardnish and have lots more babies. She sobs and sobs, saying it would make her the happiest girl in the world and that she has dreamed of it since our encounter on the train.

Blissfully happy, we head back into town. Louise chatters away like a starling while I am quiet and reflective, savouring the excitement of it all. Louise is sure that she'll be sent back to Britain with me when she tells Matron – that is what happens when nurses fall pregnant.

'Does Prissie know about the baby?' I ask.

'Of course!' Louise laughs, as if it is the natural thing for the father not to hear first. I am a bit taken aback hearing this, but I know how close the girls are.

Prissie is waiting for us when we get back. Louise and I share our excitement with her, with Louise holding my hand and jumping up and down with the thrill of it all.

Prissie has been talking to Colonel Macdonald, one of the officers in her hospital, and she's discovered that, yes, he knows a piper named Donald Peter Gillies well. He has heard all about our getting cut off from the British troops and having to make our way inland. He hadn't given us any chance of getting back alive and is keen for us to go and visit him.

'He has something for you,' Prissie says.

I am overjoyed. Colonel Macdonald saw me at my very worst, straight after I had been freed by the Scouts. He is a practical man with whom I have always felt I could discuss anything, and as a long-term ally of my father he would no doubt offer me sound advice. Prissie tells me that he has severe dysentery, and that the hospitals are very low on medicines for it – not that they were particularly effective anyway.

After Louise comes off duty the next night, we visit him. Both of us are in uniform, keen to impress.

'*Ciamar a tha thu*, DP,' he says, using the Gaelic. 'And how are you doing, laddie? Excuse me for not getting up.' He has a twinkle in his eye. 'Not dressed to receive visitors.'

He has some lemonade brought over for us and sits us down.

'Your eyes don't look too bad at all,' he says. 'And how's the shoulder?'

'Well, I'll be a one-eyed man from now on, but the other one is well on the mend,' I explain. I tell him I'm still very weak and am finding it difficult to put on weight, that the doctors have no idea what the problem is but Louise is force-feeding me.

I introduce Louise.

'Yes, your nurse friend told me about you,' he says with a friendly knowing wink. 'I have something for you, DP. You don't look right without them, somehow.' He calls out to the nurse to bring over what's in the cupboard.

It's Prissie. She comes over, opens the leather case and places my bagpipes in my arms.

I am so shocked I can hardly speak. 'What a great thing, Colonel! Thank you so much. I had not dared believe they would find their way off Suvla beach.'

I take the chanter in my hands, and finger a few silent notes.

'We'll want a tune, DP,' says the Colonel. 'Best not play in here, though. It might polish off a few of the sick. In the street outside when you leave, eh?'

'All right, sir, maybe not now. I need to get them going again. And my fingers need a bit of practice, too. I'll play Skinner's "The Lovat Scouts" the next time I see you, sir.'

'Grand. I'm glad you're here to take them, DP. I feared that I would be walking to Ardnish and giving them to your father with commiserations about your departure from this life . . . Have you heard from your parents?'

'Yes, but the last letter was written two months ago. It was all talk of me in the trenches. I've written to them, so hopefully they'll know the good news by now.'

He turns to Louise. 'And how are you, young lady? Nurse says you were looking after DP in the Casualty Clearing Station and you have been together ever since.'

Louise immediately tells him everything: about meeting me on the train in England and then looking after me, and that we are engaged and expecting a baby.

He shakes us firmly by the hand. 'There's not many good things coming out of this war,' he said. 'What splendid news.'

Everyone in the ward is smiling by this stage. 'We will have to get you married, quickly,' he says. 'Make everything legit. Are you Catholic, Louise?'

Louise shakes her head.

'Well, let me see what I can do. Come back in a couple of days.'

We leave the hospital, stunned, but it does seem the perfect solution. 'Mother, Father, meet Louise, Mrs Donald Peter Gillies . . . and we are expecting a baby.'

Two days later, we return and it is all organised. Father Tom Mullen, an army padre, is to carry out the service at a Catholic church in the town, Colonel Willie will be my best man, Prissie the bridesmaid, and it is to happen on Saturday.

I think of Sandy, how we had promised to be each other's best men.

Louise and Prissie worry about their hair and getting flowers for the church and generally get themselves wound up into a state of panic. We are both going to get married in uniform. I have only standard green military trousers issued by stores in Valletta, but the Colonel gets his hands on a Lovat Scout bonnet for me.

Several of the men who had joined me on the wall in town are there, plus three sisters from Louise's hospital, who look stunning in their scarlet-and-white uniforms. Also there is the lady who owns the room we rent. To my delight, the Colonel has found a piper – Willie Fraser, whom I know well – and as we emerge as husband and wife, he has a few choice tunes for us.

'Can you play "Cuir sa' chiste mhòir mi"?' I request, smiling at Willie, and the Colonel and I laugh uproariously.

'What does that mean? Why is it so funny?' Louise asks.

'It means "put me in the big chest",' I reply. 'There's a story behind the name. I'll tell you some other time.'

Both Louise and Prissie are crying with the excitement as we walk out and flowers are thrown over the bride by our new friends. We sit in a café and have lunch, after which we talk and drink into the early hours.

A wonderful and memorable day.

*

Louise needed to get permission from the corps to marry, but a word from the Colonel advising that she is pregnant definitely helped. They agreed that she should accompany me back to England and then hand over her uniform and be dismissed.

I continue to do not much while she works. The Lovat Scouts are back in Egypt, but they are being posted to Salonika. There is still a handful of Scouts at different hospitals, so I go around each of them and have a few words. I remember one in particular, a Sergeant McIvor from Fort William, who has had his leg amputated but is determined to walk again. He has a false leg yet strides about town as if it were his own. I am interested in his leg, as it is far better than the one my father has; it bends smoothly at the knee and seems to be much more comfortable against the stump of his thigh.

Another scout, Ewan Morrison from Invergarry, was a stalker at Glen Quoich. He has terrible injuries up one side of his body from exploding munitions and a badly scarred face, one eye missing and no arm. Yet he is desperate to get back to the Highlands and go stalking again, though I doubt if his employer will take him back.

What all the injured men have in common is their worry about how their wives or sweethearts will take their injuries. Will they be unable to cope, and leave them?

'With the huge numbers getting killed, they'll be desperate to keep you,' I reassure them. It is the best I can come up with in the circumstances.

*

There is no doubt that Gallipoli has been a terrible campaign. No land gained and over a hundred thousand allies killed. The conditions were dreadful, the rain and cold, the flooding and the terrible lack of food. In Malta I see shell-shocked soldiers wandering the streets of the town in a daze; they sit and talk to themselves, sometimes shout. As I sit with them on the wall in the warm spring sun, or meet them in the wards, much of the talk is about the futility of it all. Some say they are glad they have been injured; they couldn't have taken any more. An Australian sergeant says he will never be the same man again.

The post comes, and once again I have a couple of letters. One is from my mother:

Dear Donald Peter,

I received your letter and immediately burst into tears. The last we had heard is that you were 'missing – presumed dead' delivered in an official brown envelope. Your father was on the hill, and as he came towards the village I ran leaping up and down, like my mad collie, waving your letter. Your father has lost ten years of age and goes everywhere with a huge smile once again. Of course your eyes are a worry but it's so splendid to hear they are improving.

We are excited to hear about Louise and the great escape you have had and are so glad you will be home with us soon.

Everyone at Ardnish sends their very best and your father asks you to give his regards to Colonel Macdonald.

Send a telegram when you have details so we can be there to meet you. Will Louise be with you?

God bless and thank the Lord for your salvation.

Love your mother

I show the letter to Louise, and she puts her hand in mine. 'I am so looking forward to meeting them,' she says. 'They sound lovely.'

*

The next day there is a huge storm. It's Sunday. Louise and I are coming out of Mass and we can see the black clouds to the east.

'Quick,' she says, 'let's get home before it reaches us.'

Almost as soon as we open the door to our room, it hits. Wild gusts of wind blow everything around as we rush to close the shutters. It is terrifying, but exciting; the rain is heavier than I've ever seen and hammers noisily against the windows.

It is over as quickly as it arrived, though the street is ankle deep in water and there is a steady drip in the corner where a tile on the roof must be missing.

We're due to meet the others down at the café in the harbour so we dash down, avoiding the puddles everywhere. Everyone has a story about a big storm, and mine is about one that my father had a particular involvement with.

HOME

At home, there is a scrapbook full of old newspaper cuttings that my parents collected over the years, and the great storm of 1879 features in several from the *Oban Times* and the *Scotsman*.

My father was a young teenager and was in the house we live in now when it happened. He said it was the most frightening thing in his life – even worse than the Boer War or the time when he capsized in his boat a mile offshore.

The date was the twenty-eighth of December. He described the sudden blackening of the sky from the west. All the animals in the byre were agitated and making a lot of noise, and the dogs were brought into the house, when they would normally be outside. My grandfather shouted to my grandmother, 'Get the children inside, shut all the doors and make sure the hens and sheds are all right. Warn the neighbours. I'm going down to tie up the boats a bit better. It's going to be an evil one by the look of things.'

At that time of the year it was dark by four, anyway. They sat in the front room with the weather getting worse and worse outside. The door rattled and creaked; they could feel a wind in the house so strong it was if there were no windows. The house was soon leaking like a sieve; everything was soaked.

My grandfather went out the back door about six to see if the animals were fine and to check up on the older people in the village.

He came back drenched, as if he had just been for a swim, with a look of panic. 'It's chaos,' he reported. 'Archie Macdonald's house has lost its roof so he and Kirsty have gone to the MacEachans. The hen house is nowhere to be seen, and one of the boats is up across the front of the byre. It's so heavy I couldn't move it an inch myself. Blown uphill from the beach for two hundred yards! Just shows what a gale we are having. I was blown clean off my feet, landed about six feet away. The heather thatch on our roof has come off completely; it's just the wood that's screwed on that's holding.'

My father told me that his parents talked about what to do if the roof came off and where they might be safest. They agreed on the woodshed. Its entrance faced away from the wind, and it had stone slabs on the roof.

Grandfather pulled out his missal and read to the family. They genuinely felt that the end of the world was upon them.

After three or four hours, the storm stopped suddenly. The wind dropped, and my grandfather and father went outside with an oil lamp to survey the damage. Everyone in Peanmeanach took shelter in the driest house and came out to see the chaos at dawn. The boats were matchsticks; all the houses had lost their thatch; the schoolhouse was without its slate roof, with tiles found on the hill five hundred yards away. The hill cattle had taken shelter behind a bank, but one of them had been blown over and broken its back. The men slaughtered and butchered it that day.

The *Oban Times* articles were full of stories about the Corpach pier being destroyed in the worst hurricane in living memory and trees down in their tens of thousands across the west coast. All the fishing boats were destroyed – a catastrophe for the men in the area as they were the main source of living. Apparently, Jemima Blackburn replaced them, using the profits from her paintings.

It was the night of the Tay Bridge disaster, when the longest bridge in the world blew down with a train full of people on it.

WAR

In the evenings, Louise and I wander the streets. Malta is known as 'the Nurse of the Mediterranean' because so many of the injured are brought here. There are always lots of people bustling around the docks and the streets of the town, enjoying the evening sun. Locals, too, but mostly soldiers – Anzacs, with their ready smiles and powerful physiques. Indian and African soldiers, every colour and shape and almost all with bandages or crutches.

We share a glass of wine with the nurses and my friends on the wall and return, contented, to our room. Louise says she has never been happier in her life: she's with the man she loves, expecting his baby, in a place of our own, in a beautiful part of the world and with so much to look forward to. My parents will be hoeing the recently planted oats and potatoes, no doubt struggling with the hard work. The thought of it pains me. I am desperate to get back to help with the harvest and enjoy the summer – the best time of the year in the west.

*

It is Louise who sees the packet in a shop window. The label reads: 'Dr Sheridan's Remedy. A Sure Cure for Dysentery'. Horrified, she buys one and brings it home to show me. We decide that the best course of action is for her to see Colonel Thomas at the Queen Alexandra HQ and tell her of our suspicions. But first, she decides to go around the island and see how widely available it is.

She discovers that it is readily available: most shops are stocking it and it is selling well, according to the shopkeepers. She asks them what Dr Sheridan looks like.

'Tall, dark hair, academic-looking, wears a smart white coat,' they report. 'Always introduces himself as a doctor.'

'Sounds like our man,' we agree.

She and Prissie go to the hospital and wait for an hour to see Colonel Thomas. She is one of the most senior officers in the entire corps and will surely be able to help. They tell her about their encounter with Dr Sheridan on the way out from England, his complete lack of knowledge and incompetence at the hospital, and of the time that Matron had to conduct an operation while he was out of the room.

Colonel Thomas takes the packet, opens it and sniffs the contents.

'We were sure he was a fraud – everyone was,' Prissie says.

They tell her about Mr Bustin, the engineer on the ship on their outward journey, who had been going to write to two Harley Street doctors he knew and ask them to check if Sheridan was qualified, and to let the head of the army medical team in Turkey know.

The Colonel writes everything down, and says she'll look into it and that they have done the right thing coming to her.

The girls leave, feeling confident that Dr Sheridan will at last be revealed as a fraudster and that justice will be served.

'I'll bet he puts the same rotten stuff in packets saying it's a cure for the common cold as well as the plague,' sniffs Prissie. 'I wonder if he's here on the island. Maybe we'll meet him and he'll know it was us who reported him! Frankly, I don't care.'

*

We learn the next day that places have been found for Louise and me on the *Gloucester Castle*. We'll be heading back next week. A sheer coincidence that this is the same ship that Louise and Prissie had worked on when docked off Suvla Bay. Louise is now four months' pregnant and keen to sail before she gets too big and uncomfortable. As we will be on a hospital ship, we can be fairly sure of a safe passage.

Colonel Willie is heading across to Egypt soon, to rejoin the Scouts, so only Prissie will remain in Malta. She insists she's very happy about it, though. There are a lot worse places she could be, with the summer coming and all these handsome officers around to entertain her.

Louise and I discuss our plans for home. After handing in our papers, we'll go to see Louise's mother, who Louise hasn't seen since she qualified – more than eight months ago. And Owen, too; Louise is excited to see how he's faring. We then plan to leave the Valleys and head directly to Scotland – to my beloved Ardnish.

*

During our last week in Malta, I have plenty of time to read my letters again.

I love the two from Angus. He had signed up to join the Lovat Scouts, but they didn't a need a padre, so a year ago he was assigned to the Cameron Highlanders, who were based at Fort George, Blair Atholl, and then Aberfeldy in Perthshire. They were training to go to France and were camped in the grounds of Castle Menzies. He was billeted with a farming family, the MacDiarmids, who live nearby. They are great pipers and spent many happy hours introducing each other to new tunes and learning an especially difficult pibroch together. To think, there might be only two people, apart from our father, who can play it now! Father has always been keen for me to learn it; it is important that we keep it going, and now my brother has learned it before me!

After rifle drill and fitness training, they would practise river crossings over the Tay, which inevitably would end up with some swimming. Those days were glorious, he reported, with plenty of opportunity to fish on one of the great rivers of Scotland. He had considerable success and seldom returned without a fish or two to supplement their rations.

From there, he had gone to Struan and then by train to Glasgow. He had caught up with Aunt Aggy and had seen some of the priests he'd taken his vows with. They spent a week there, waiting for a ship which took them down to Le Havre in France to join the 2nd battalion. From there, it was on to Salonika, arriving just before Christmas; when Louise, Prissie and I had been making our way through Turkey near Kesan.

*

Sadly, Louise has no letters from her mother. Her mother had never learned to read or write, although Louise had written to her several times since we had arrived in Malta, hoping that a friend would read them to her. She had decided not to reveal anything to her mother in writing, other than she has a man in her life. She wants our news to be a treat.

*

'They've arrested Dr Sheridan!' Prissie cries, 'just this morning! I saw him coming out of St Andrew's Hospital and I ran and told the Queen Alexandra Superintendent. They called the Military Police and he's been locked up!'

She takes my hands and jumps up and down with excitement. 'I have to go and tell Louise!' And with that, she's off.

That evening, the three of us get together and celebrate.

It had been eight months since they first identified him as a charlatan, and there had been times when we thought he would get away scot free. We raise our glasses and toast his downfall, glad that we are still here. If it had happened even a few days later, we might never have heard.

I feel very proud of the girls' actions.

*

Prissie and Colonel Willie come to the quayside to see us off.

Louise is close to tears and hugs her friend for a long time. 'You have to come and see us as soon as you get leave. We want you to be Godmother.'

Prissie bursts into tears, too. Colonel Willie, who is sailing in the next day or two, clasps my hand. 'Good luck, DP, and give my best to your father. Remember to keep at the piping. I'm looking forward to hearing you play at the Scouts' lunch in Fort William.'

*

We arrive in Southampton on a grey damp day at the end of April. The passengers line the deck as the ship steams past the Isle of Wight; we watch sailing boats coming out to escort us in and enjoy the din of the ferries and bigger boats sounding their horns in welcome. Louise has to go straight to London to hand in her uniform, and I have to sign on for my disability pension. It wouldn't be enough to have a great life, but we certainly wouldn't starve. Louise will have to work, too, that's for sure. I kiss her goodbye at the station and return to barracks in Southampton where I am billeted for a few days. I see an army doctor about my eyes and enjoy the weather.

When Louise returns from London, she is rather downcast.

'I was so sad to hand in my uniform, DP. I was really proud of it. Coming from the Valleys, it was the first time I earned real respect. When people saw me in my scarlet and white, I could see they thought, here's someone with knowledge, with gravitas. I'll miss that.'

I squeeze her tightly and reassure her that she still has knowledge and gravitas – as well as beauty.

We take the train to Abergavenny to surprise Louise's mum, and wait outside the hospital for her to come out. There are squeals of delight at first, until I am introduced. I see the woman's face fall. What sort of success was this, bringing home a half-blind and emaciated ex-soldier?

The feeling is mutual. I see a prematurely aged woman with greasy hair, puckered lips, a permanent frown and a life that has been shaped by disappointment. How can she be my beautiful Louise's mother?

She isn't impressed to see that Louise is pregnant, either. 'You didn't bide your time there, girl,' she says coldly. She is reluctant to take us to her home, but Louise isn't going anywhere else. As soon as we cross the threshold we see why. The dirty dishes are piled high in the sink, and the place hasn't been cleaned in months.

I meet Daffie, the dog I'd heard so much about. Louise makes a real fuss of him. He's too fat and needs exercise. All the furniture is chewed. I tell Louise that it's no good for a collie to be shut in like this.

Louise's mother has a new man in her life – David – who we don't take to at all. He is a wee man, dirty and shifty. He had dodged conscription, pleading sickness, and is unemployed. He stays with us for half an hour before announcing he has to go to the pub to meet 'the boys'.

Louise has a ferocious row with her mother about him. 'You can do better than him, Mam. You'd be better off without him. And what about Owen? How is all this good for him?'

'You can hardly talk, young lady,' she snaps. 'The first man you meet and you're in his bed and pregnant!'

Both women are in tears, barely able to look at each other. I decide to find somewhere for us to stay that night. There is little to choose from, but eventually I find a boarding house. It is noisy, dirty and overpriced. The food is inedible, just watery brown soup and stale bread.

'This doesn't compare well with Malta, does it, DP?' Louise says mournfully. 'Wine, fish, salad, sunshine and friends all around us.'

We lie in silence, legs intertwined on the narrow bed, and try not to think about what a disappointment our return home is proving to be.

'Mam knows perfectly well that David's not a good sort,' says Louise. 'She loved Dad, even at the end when he was so horrible to her. She's the sort who needs someone around, and David is that someone.'

I can't help thinking her mum is no great catch, either.

'Let's take Owen with us,' I suggest. 'And the dog. Let's go straight to Ardnish! It doesn't cost much to live there, we can get an empty house from the estate, and my war pension will do us for a while. You can make some money like my mother does. Owen will grow up with the sea, the lochs, the hills. There's fresh air and a good education up there. He'll be like a brother to our baby. My family would welcome him in.'

Louise contemplates this and asks lots of questions. Would he get to go to school? What work would he do when he was older? I try to be as honest as I can.

Eventually she decides: 'You're right, DP. It's a great idea. It would be good for Owen. Let's ask him.'

The next day, we meet Owen as he is coming home from school. We sit and talk. He is a nice lad, just a bit withdrawn and reluctant to talk. He hates David, his mother is depressed, and school isn't going well as a result. Owen quickly agrees that he wants to come with us, that it will be the right thing for him to do.

'Your mother has to agree, though,' I tell him. 'We can't just take you away from her. But we can tell her she can come and visit.' I look across at Louise, who nods her agreement.

And so, everything is agreed. Mam knows that Owen and David will never get on, and it's not hard to convince her that Owen will have a better life with us. She doesn't say as much, but we can tell that is what she is thinking.

Louise's other brother Thomas comes from Merthyr Tydfil to meet us at the Station Hotel, and we eat together with Louise's mother and Owen. Thankfully, I get on with Thomas. We're not too different in age, and he promises to come and visit in the summer with his mother. We all agree that if Owen isn't happy, then he'll come back with them then.

I send a telegram my parents: 'Arrive Tuesday 3.15 train, DP' is all it says.

The army has given warrants for my wife and me to get the train back to Lochailort, and so with Owen, Daffie, bagpipes and luggage we set off, bound for Crewe and then Glasgow.

The train belches sparks and steam as it trundles through Wales towards the north and a new beginning for my family. Louise clings on to my arm and watches as Owen's confidence gradually grows. His eyes are huge with excitement as he absorbs all the sights unfolding along the track.

I tell the boy about the life we'll have when we got there and how he'll be made welcome by the friendly people on Ardnish. He can fish for lobsters, help with the deer stalking, the harvest – everything.

'You'll love it, Owen, but it'll be nothing like your life in Wales.'

From Crewe onwards, we are in darkness. Louise lies fast asleep on my lap. I can feel the bump of the baby; it's quite big now. I am a lucky man to have found this girl. I doze happily, thinking of Ardnish, my family and how well things have turned out. I know my mother will fall in love with Louise and be as excited about the baby as we are.

In Glasgow, there are crowds of raucous soldiers waiting for trains. The babble of voices competes to be heard over the noise of the engines. We have to change stations to get on the West Highland Line, and we are cutting it fine to catch the only onward train of the day. The rain is pelting down. Daffie's pulling at his lead, and my bagpipes and suitcase keep slipping from my grip. Louise and Owen are close behind me. We'll just make it and no more . . .

LOUISE

Only a few minutes, and we'll be on the train north. I can't wait. This hustle and bustle isn't for me; Ardnish sounds more my sort of place.

'Wait for me, DP!' I call out.

I am only a few feet behind him, a bag in each hand, struggling to keep up. I jostle through the throng, and then lose sight of him. I stop to look around, trying to pick him out in the crowd.

A tram bell rings, and I hear a sickening thud. A moment of deathly silence, and then a woman screams.

Somehow, I know it's DP. I push forward and see him there on the ground, his body twisted, motionless. A pool of blood oozes onto the rain-soaked cobbles. Daffie's straining at the lead, which is wrapped tightly around DP's lifeless hand.

*

Two days pass in a blur. The authorities agree that my husband's body should be sent by train to Lochailort. I know it's the right thing to do. He would want to be buried alongside his family.

By now I am determined to go to Ardnish . . .

*

HOME

The two old boatmen speak Gaelic in hushed tones. The oars dip and pull, causing barely a ripple on the water. I am perched at the rear of the boat looking straight ahead; Owen is hanging over the bow looking at starfish.

It is exactly as he described. Beautiful cattle with enormous curved horns and hair the colour of DP's stand down by the shore. The grass is a vibrant green, the rocks are glistening from a recent shower, and the air is alive with birdsong.

The sun drops in the sky. Suddenly, I can hear DP's voice in my head telling me why this peninsula, with its curving beach and towering mountains opposite reflected in the sea, is the most beautiful place on earth. One of the men turns to me and points, and there, just coming into view, is a bay with its crescent of thatched cottages.

Smoke is wafting from the chimneys, and the glow of the setting sun makes everything seem warm and welcoming. I can see three figures in the distance. It's them – Morag and Donald and Father Angus.

I breathe deeply, smooth a hand over my hair and compose myself. I'm ready to meet them, to tell them their beloved son has died and I am bearing his child. With Owen and Daffie beside me, I climb out of the boat and walk across the beach towards Ardnish and home.

Author's Note

Ardnish Was Home is a work of fiction. Names, characters, places, events and incidents are either products of the author's imagination or used in a fictitious manner. While some of the names are those of real people who lived at the time the novel is set, what they did and said has been fabricated.